MW01137068

Made in Savannah
Cozy Mystery Series Book Ten

Hope
Callaghan

hopecallaghan.com
Copyright © 2018
All rights reserved.

*****

Visit my website for new releases and special offers: hopecallaghan.com

Thank you to these wonderful ladies who help make my books shine - Peggy H., Cindi G., Jean P., Wanda D., Barbara W. and Renate P. for taking the time to preview *Pirates in Peril,* for the extra sets of eyes and for catching all of my mistakes.

A special THANKS to my reader review teams, here in the U.S., and those across the pond, over the border and an ocean away!

Alice, Amary, Barbara, Becky, Becky B., Brinda, Cassie, Charlene, Christina, Deb, Debbie, Dee, Denota, Devan, Grace, Jan, Jo-Ann, Joeline, Joyce, Jean K., Jean M., Katherine, Lynne, Megan, Melda, Kat, Linda, Lynne, Pat, Patsy, Paula, Rebecca, Rita, Tamara, Valerie and Vicki.

Allie, Anca, Angela, Ann, Anne, Bev, Bobbi, Bonny, Carol, Carmen, David, Debbie, Diana, Elaine, Elizabeth, Gareth, Ingrid, Jane, Jayne, Jean, Joan, Karen, Kate, Kathy, Lesley, Margaret, Marlene, Patricia, Pauline, Sharon, Sheila and Susan.

Contents

Cast of Characters

Carlita Garlucci. The widow of a mafia "made" man, Carlita promised her husband on his deathbed to get their sons out of the "family" business, so she moves from New York to the historic city of Savannah, Georgia. But escaping the family isn't as easy as she hoped it would be and trouble follows Carlita to her new home.

Mercedes Garlucci. Carlita's daughter and the first to move to Savannah with her mother. An aspiring writer, Mercedes has a knack for finding mysteries and adventure.

Vincent Garlucci, Jr. Carlita's oldest son and a younger version of his father, Vinnie is deeply entrenched in the "family business" and is not interested in leaving New York.

Tony Garlucci. Carlita's middle son and the first to follow his mother to Savannah. Tony is protective of both his mother and his sister, which is a good thing since the Garlucci women are always in some sort of a predicament.

Paulie Garlucci. Carlita's youngest son. Mayor of the small town of Clifton Falls, NY, Paulie never joined the "family business," and is content to live his life with his wife and young children far away from a life of crime. Gina, Paulie's wife, rules the family household with an iron fist.

Chapter 1

Mercedes stepped inside the apartment. She slinked past an oversized armoire blocking her path and reached for the handle of her Segway.

"You're in the way," a deep male voice growled from the stairwell.

"Give me a sec." Mercedes tugged on the handle, firmly wedged behind the large piece of bedroom furniture. "I'll be out of here as soon as I move this out of the way."

"It shouldn't be parked there in the first place when someone is trying to move in. You'll have to leave it 'til later. There's no way to get it out right now."

Mercedes could feel her blood begin to boil as she lifted her gaze, her eyes locking with the most unusual combination of blue-green eyes. The man arched his brow, his lip curling at the corners in a mocking smirk.

"I wasn't aware a *tenant* was moving in today." Mercedes added extra emphasis to the word tenant and crossed her arms as she forced herself to defy the unpleasant man who was staring down at her. "A little notice would have been appreciated and I certainly would have moved my Segway to a safer spot."

The stairs creaked as the man slowly descended the steps, making his way past the armoire until he was standing mere inches from Mercedes, who was trapped in the corner. "Mrs. Garlucci was aware I was moving in. Are you the cleaning lady?"

"Cleaning lady?" Mercedes sputtered. A hot heat burned up her neck. "I'm Mercedes Garlucci, part owner of this property."

The statement was a bit of a stretch. Technically, Mercedes' mother, Carlita, was the sole owner of 210 Mulberry Street, a restored apartment building in Savannah's beautiful and historic Walton Square.

"Huh." The man crossed his arms, mimicking Mercedes' stance.

The duo continued their stare down for several long seconds, until Mercedes' palm itched with the overwhelming desire to slap the smirk off the stranger's face.

Certain her mother would be furious, not to mention the sneaking suspicion the action would somehow cause her opponent to emerge the victor, she quickly changed tactics and forced a smile. "If you would be so kind as to back up, I'll get out of your way."

The man took a step back, giving Mercedes a wide berth to slip past him. She was almost in the clear when he abruptly stepped forward, as if he was going to block her again.

"Pfft." Mercedes bolted past him and picked up the pace, taking the stairs two at a time. She

could feel the heat of his stare as his eyes bore into her back. "Jerk," she hissed under her breath as she flung the apartment door open.

She stormed into the apartment, slamming the hall door so hard, the pictures hanging on the wall rattled.

Startled by the loud bang, Carlita Garlucci spun in her chair and clutched her chest. "For Pete's sake, Mercedes. Please don't slam the door. You scared the daylights out of me."

"Sorry, Ma." Mercedes marched across the room. "That man is making my blood boil."

"I know your brother can be aggravating at times, but you two need to learn to walk away from each other when you disagree."

"I'm not talking about Tony." Mercedes jabbed her finger toward the door. "It's the rude, arrogant, egotistical, self-important tenant across the hall."

Carlita frowned. "Are you talking about Mr. Ivey, our new tenant? He's such a nice young man. Earlier this morning, he saw me struggling with my bags of groceries and helped me carry them to the apartment. Now there's a real gentleman."

"Not to me. I noticed there was furniture in the downstairs hall, so I thought I would be nice and move my Segway to make more room. The jerk had the nerve to get onto me about leaving my stuff in the way."

"I'm sorry, Mercedes. I forgot to tell you Mr. Ivey was moving in today. It completely slipped my mind after Bob Lowman caught me in the alley to go over some details for the new apartment."

Mercedes shuffled across the room. "Did Tony and Shelby approve the final reno changes?"

Tony, Carlita's middle son, had recently become engaged to Shelby Townsend, one of Carlita's tenants. Tony currently lived in a small efficiency on the lower level behind Savannah Swag, the pawnshop Carlita and her children owned. Shelby rented a two bedroom, one bath apartment across the hall.

The couple planned to move into a larger place, one where they would have room to expand their family and give Violet, Shelby's daughter, siblings.

Carlita came up with the idea to add a larger apartment above the adjacent building, which would house Ravello, Carlita's restaurant. The timing was perfect.

Since Ravello was close to being finished, Lowman's crew was able to start working on the three bedroom, two-bath unit. The new apartment would be ready in time for the couple's summer wedding, giving the family of three a new home to start their new life.

"Yes." Carlita slowly nodded. "The apartment is coming along nicely. Which reminds me..." She slipped her reading glasses on and turned her attention to the computer screen. "I need to start running some ads to rent out Tony's efficiency and Shelby's apartment before the wedding."

"I'll let you handle the ads if you let me screen the tenants," Mercedes muttered. "We don't need another Sam Ivey moving in. One is enough."

Carlita jotted a reminder note on her to-do list. "I'm sorry you two got off on the wrong foot. Once Mr. Ivey settles in, I'll invite him to dinner, so we can all get better acquainted."

"Remind me not to be here." Mercedes walked into the kitchen and poured a glass of lemonade. "I thought you were supposed to meet Pirate Pete and Tori this afternoon."

"Fudge! I completely forgot." Carlita sprang from her chair and jogged to her bedroom.

"You forgot?" Mercedes trailed behind her mother. "You've been talking about this meeting all week."

"I know." Carlita grabbed her purse and hurried to the door. "Pete and Tori are excited about this new venture, but I'm not sure I can handle another business. Once Ravello is up and running, we'll have our hands full running the restaurant and the pawnshop, not to mention being a landlord."

"You might want to take the fire escape instead," Mercedes joked. "Getting by our new tenant on the stairs is going to be impossible."

"Mercedes," her mother chided. "You need to give Sam Ivey a chance."

"I think he hates me and he doesn't even know me."

Carlita stepped into the hall and Mercedes joined her. "Good luck at your meeting. Maybe Tori and Pete are looking for a silent partner."

"I'll find out soon enough. We're meeting at Pete's place. I'll be back a little later." Carlita sidestepped two men, who were carrying a couch up the stairs.

The new tenant stood at the bottom of the stairs, directing the movers. When Carlita reached the landing, she stopped to chat.

She could hear the tinkle of her mother's laughter and Ivey's low voice. He chuckled and patted Carlita's arm before she stepped out of the building. Mercedes quickly slipped back inside the apartment, anxious to avoid another confrontation.

Carlita pulled the door shut behind her and then hurried to the sidewalk.

When she reached the entrance to the Parrot House, she stopped to catch her breath before stepping into the restaurant's lobby and making her way to the hostess station. "Yes, I'm looking for Pete. I have a meeting with him at two o'clock."

"Mrs. Garlucci?" The young woman smiled.

"Yes."

"Follow me."

Carlita followed the woman through the dining room and down a long hall to a door marked "Private."

The woman rapped lightly before twisting the knob and leaning in. "Mrs. Garlucci is here."

"Have her come in," Pirate Pete's booming voice echoed into the hall.

The young woman waited until Carlita was inside before closing the door behind her.

Pirate Pete made his way around the front of the desk to give Carlita a quick hug. She caught the faint smell of an expensive cigar mingled with an earthy cologne. The cologne reminded her of a scent Carlita's deceased husband, Vinnie, had worn.

"I hope I'm not late."

Gunner, Pete's parrot, began to squawk. "You're late."

"Carlita is not late," Pirate Pete scolded. "Mind your manners."

"Gunner is handsome," Gunner replied.

Carlita wandered over to the parrot's cage. "Gunner is handsome. I'm sorry I'm late."

"Time to walk the plank."

"Maybe later," Carlita chuckled.

"You're not late and if Gunner doesn't watch it, I'm going to cover his cage."

"No!" Gunner screeched. "Don't cover the cage."

"Then behave yourself." Pete motioned to the empty chair next to Tori. "Tori just got here, too."

"Hello, Carlita. I was just telling Pete I'm thrilled you're interested in our potential business venture."

"I have my hands full with the pawnshop, the apartment rentals and soon, Ravello, my new restaurant, but I'm always open to new ideas." Carlita settled into the seat and set her purse on the floor next to her. "I have to admit, I'm dying to hear what you two have up your sleeves."

"Good!" Tori's eyes twinkled. She turned to Pirate Pete, who resumed his place behind the desk. "I'll let you tell Carlita what we have, as she says, 'up our sleeves.'"

Chapter 2

Pete cleared his throat. "As you know, Tori and I have been tossing around the idea of doing something with the gems you shared with us, the ones you recovered from your property. Savannah is a booming tourist town. Restaurants are a good investment, but they're a lot of work."

"Plus, you already got one," Carlita said.

"Right." Pirate Pete continued. "Because our area is a top tourist destination, I thought - what better way to invest our money than to combine all of our expertise to treat tourists to something special, something they can't get anywhere else?"

"At least not in Savannah," Tori said. "I'm sure you heard the talk about a casino gambling boat."

"You could say that," Carlita said. She didn't mention her son, Vinnie, along with Vinnie's new father-in-law, recently visited to explore the gambling boat venture.

"We certainly weren't interested in opening a gambling boat because it brings in a certain criminal element," Tori said.

"You have no idea," Carlita mumbled. "So what have you come up with?"

"A pirate ship," Pete said.

"A pirate ship?" Carlita wrinkled her nose. "Where do you get a pirate ship?"

"I have a friend who lives in Florida, over in the Bay Area. He owns a pirate boat and says business is booming, so I took a trip down there. I was impressed by the success of his pirate ship and after checking it out, I thought why not? I already have a pirate restaurant, why not a pirate ship?"

"Where do I fit in? I don't know anything about the pirate business. Mafia? Check. Pirate? No."

"But Pete does," Tori said. "The Savannah gambling boat is already in the works and has pretty much paved the way for more riverfront business ventures."

"What if the city doesn't approve a pirate ship venture?" Carlita was painfully aware of all of the red tape involved in starting a business, not to mention obtaining permits and business licenses.

"The permit is already in place." Tori winked at Carlita. "It pays to have connections. Now all we have to do is wait for our ship to come in."

"Very funny." Carlita shifted in her chair. "How...much does a pirate ship cost?"

"Tori and I already ponied up the money. The ship is, as Tori said, on its way."

"Where do I fit in?"

"We need cash," Pete said bluntly. "We spent most of our money on the ship. Now we need some money to get the business up and running."

"We still need to hire workers, lease the dock space and pay for advertising." Tori rattled off the list. "Both you and I would be more of silent partners. Pete plans to handle the day-to-day operations."

"I have an agreement already drawn up." Pete reached for a file folder on his desk and handed it to Carlita. "We don't need an answer today. I think you should take it home and go over it, have your kids go over it."

"As well as an attorney," Tori said. "Regardless of whether you want to join us in the venture, our friendship is of utmost importance."

Victoria, aka "Tori" Montgomery and Carlita had become friends after Elvira went missing and she discovered her tenant was hiding out on

Tybee Island, searching for gems. Elvira snuck onto Tori's property, was taken down by Tori's guard dog and promptly arrested.

After Carlita helped smooth things over, Tori, along with Pirate Pete, invited her to lunch, which was the beginning of the trio's unique friendship.

Carlita glanced at the folder. "It sounds intriguing. Won't we be butting heads with the casino boat owners? Some of those casino owners can be ruthless."

Vito Castellini, her son Vinnie's father-in-law, instantly came to mind.

"The customers would be two completely different sets of clientele. I'm certain Savannah is big enough to support both businesses," Pete said confidently. "I've done my research. I believe we have an excellent chance to run a successful tourist venture and make some money."

"I'll give this serious consideration," Carlita promised. She had another sudden thought. "I wonder what the owners of the new riverboat, the Mystic Dream, will think when a pirate ship shows up on the shores of the Savannah River." The riverboat, a Savannah landmark, had recently been sold and renamed. The new owners had added small cabins and there was talk of offering overnight trip packages.

Tori and Pete exchanged a quick glance.

"You already know?"

"Lawson Bates, who also happens to be Mayor Clarence Puckett's cousin, owns the Mystic Dream." Pirate Pete told Carlita he met with Lawson and even toured the Mystic Dream. "After the tour ended, I mentioned to Lawson my idea of bringing a pirate themed boat to the shores of the Savannah River."

"And he wasn't as thrilled with the idea as you thought he would be," Carlita guessed.

"Lawson threatened to toss Pete off the side of the boat," Tori said.

"He's not keen on the competition."

"You could say that." Pirate Pete leaned back in his chair. "We exchanged a few words. I lost my cool and said some things. I hoped Lawson would see that there was room enough for all of us."

"I'm sure Lawson heard all about the gambling boat and is concerned they will be invading his turf," Tori said.

"Now we come along and he's feeling the heat," Carlita said. "I don't know Lawson Bates. I do know the mayor. He seems like a reasonable man."

"Clarence is a decent man," Tori agreed. "A fair man, if you will. We may hit a little resistance with Lawson moving forward with our venture."

"It won't be the first time for me," Carlita said.

Tori stood. "I hate to rush, but I need to get going. Byron will be here to pick me up at two-thirty."

Carlita followed Tori out of the office and Pirate Pete brought up the rear. "I would like to take a day or so to look over the papers before I give you an answer."

"Certainly, Carlita. We would expect nothing less," Pete replied.

"You must bring Violet around to the house one of these days," Tori said. "Byron has asked several times when the two of you will be by for tea."

"Violet would love to see Byron." Carlita pressed a hand to her forehead. "Oh my goodness! I forgot to tell you. Tony, my middle son, and Shelby, Violet's mother, got engaged."

"Congratulations," Tori said. "When do they plan to marry?"

"This summer. They haven't worked out all of the details yet. I'm sure it will be a small, intimate affair." Although Carlita wasn't certain of that. She hadn't had a chance to discuss the wedding with Shelby.

"You're welcome to have the wedding at Montgomery Hall," Tori offered. "I have plenty of room."

"Thank you for the generous offer," Carlita said. "I'll mention it to Tony and Shelby."

"There's also a large reception room here at the Parrot House," Pete said.

"Or we could have it aboard a pirate ship," Carlita joked.

"That we could," Pete opened the entrance door and the trio stepped onto the porch. "Thanks for meeting with us to listen to our idea. Tori and I both agree you would make the perfect third partner."

"I promise I will give it some serious consideration," Carlita said. "And if I were ever to go in on a business venture, it would be with you two."

"There's Byron." Tori waved as Byron, her driver, steered the sedan into the parking lot.

He exited the driver's side and opened the rear passenger door before joining them. "Mrs. Garlucci, Mr. Taylor."

"Hello, Byron. How are you?"

"Splendid. It's a beautiful day. Did Miss Tori invite you to tea?"

"I did," Tori answered.

"Yes, she did." Carlita nodded. "She invited me and asked if Violet wanted to come along."

A slow smile crept across Byron's face. "I know you're busy, but I sure would like to see Violet someday soon."

"And I'm sure she would love to see you, too." Carlita patted the file folder she was holding. "I'll get with Tori in the next day or so. I need to meet with her again anyway."

Byron nodded and the smile never left his face as he helped Tori into the car before returning to the driver's side.

Carlita waited for the car to drive off before turning her attention to Pete. "When do you take possession of your pirate ship?"

"The ship is on the way. It will be here any day now. As soon as it arrives, I'll arrange to take you and Tori on a grand tour."

"I would like that," Carlita said.

"I fear Lawson Bates may try to pull some strings and undermine our business venture before it ever sets sail." A flicker of concern crossed Pete's face.

"Is there a chance his cousin will side with him?"

"I don't know. You know the saying...blood is thicker than water."

"If that happens, we'll fight it," Carlita vowed. "And if that doesn't work, I know a few people up north who might be able to help us out."

Pete chuckled. "I hope it doesn't come to that. Looking back, perhaps I shoulda done a little more investigating before ordering the pirate ship."

"But you have the necessary permits," Carlita pointed out. "Competition is a good thing. I predict Lawson Bates will eventually come around."

"Or not and make all of our lives miserable," Pete said.

Carlita waved the file folder. "I'll be back in touch in a couple of days." She thanked Pete again for including her and then slowly walked home.

Despite her words of confidence to Pete, and Tori's connections, she was concerned the pirate boat wouldn't hit the high seas.

She knew Mayor Puckett in passing. What if the mayor managed to pull some strings and he permanently grounded the pirate ship?

If they couldn't get the business up and running, who in the world would want to purchase a pirate ship? It was something Carlita needed to consider.

When Carlita returned home, she found a note from Mercedes telling her mother she had an important errand to run and after that, planned to meet Autumn for a late lunch at a restaurant in the City Market district.

Carlita slipped her reading glasses on and began mulling over the agreement. Most of it was mumbo jumbo. She would need to have someone with a lot more expertise in legal agreements take a look at the papers.

The rest of the afternoon dragged by, and Mercedes' lunch date with Autumn turned into an afternoon and evening date, leaving Carlita rambling around the apartment.

She polished off some leftover lasagna and then settled in front of the television to watch the news. Carlita was still sitting there when Mercedes finally returned home looking none too happy.

"Our new tenant is going to get an earful from me the next time I see him," Mercedes fumed.

Carlita set the remote in her lap. "What happened now?"

"He left a pile of *Welcome to Savannah* signs in the spot where I park my Segway. I had to leave it in the pawnshop because there was nowhere else to put it."

"We'll ask him nicely to move the signs tomorrow," Carlita said.

"Or I can go over there right now and tell him to move his crap out of my way." Mercedes reached for the doorknob.

"Mercedes! You will not. We cannot have you and the new tenant waging war from day one. You two will make peace tomorrow or else."

Mercedes almost asked "or else what?" but judging by the tone in her mother's voice, she decided it wasn't the right reply. "Fine. I'm going to my room to work on my new murder novel. Thanks to our new tenant, I've already picked out the name of the thug, soon to be a dead guy."

"I'll take a wild guess...Sam?"

"Sam Slimey."

"Mercedes."

"Kidding, but maybe not," Mercedes mumbled under her breath. She changed the subject. "What happened during your meeting with Pirate Pete and Tori? What's the big venture?"

"A pirate ship," Carlita said.

"For real?" Mercedes' eyes widened. "We're going to be part owners of a pirate ship?"

"I don't think it's a real pirate ship, but a replica." Carlita told her daughter about the meeting and that the pirate ship was on its way to Savannah. "We would be more of a money partner than a working partner since we have our hands full with this place, not to mention we'll be even busier once Ravello opens."

"I wouldn't mind volunteering to work on board the ship." Mercedes warmed to the idea. "Think about it...I could get a killer pirate costume, a sword and come up with some cool pirate lore."

"I'm sure Pete would love the extra help." Carlita motioned toward her desk. "The agreement is on my desk. I tried to read it, but gave up."

"I can take a look at it for you, Ma. We should have Tony and maybe an attorney to look at it, too." Mercedes grabbed the folder and flipped it open. "How much are they looking for you to invest?"

28

"I don't know. I didn't see a dollar figure."

Mercedes tucked the folder under her arm. "It's only a coupla pages. I'll see if I can make heads or tails of it."

She would look at the papers just as soon as she plotted out the death of her new character, Sam Slimey, a slow, painful and torturous death, for sure.

Carlita could hear Mercedes pounding away on her keyboard when she went to bed a couple of hours later and was relieved her daughter hadn't followed through on her threat to confront their new tenant.

The next morning, she woke early and tiptoed into the kitchen to start a pot of coffee. Mercedes emerged from her room and followed her mother into the kitchen.

"What are you doing up so early?"

"I have a surprise." Mercedes covered her mouth to stifle her yawn. "What time is it?"

"Early." Carlita squinted her eyes. "Six-thirty."

"Oh! We gotta get ready. Quick!"

"At six-thirty in the morning?"

"Yes. You go throw some clothes on. I'll take Rambo out for a quick walk and then I'll meet you downstairs at six-fifty." Before Carlita could reply, Mercedes ran into the bathroom. She emerged, dressed in sweats and a t-shirt, in record time.

Carlita stared at her daughter in disbelief. "I can't remember the last time you were up this early." She pressed a hand to her daughter's forehead. "Are you feeling all right?"

"I'm fine." Mercedes swatted her mother's hand away. "I have a special surprise for you. We're gonna miss it if you don't hurry up and get dressed."

"If you say so." Carlita hurried to the bathroom to dress while Mercedes herded

Rambo out of the apartment. She threw on some jeans and a blouse, ran a comb through her hair and after a quick brush of her teeth, met her daughter in the first floor hall.

"Let's go." Mercedes flung the door open, motioning to her mother.

"Where are we going?"

"To the corner." Mercedes and her mother stopped when they reached the end of the block.

"What are we doing?"

"Waiting for the trolley."

Carlita shook her head. "The trolley doesn't stop here. The only stop around here is in front of the Parrot House."

"Not anymore," Mercedes singsonged and pointed at a trolley sign Carlita had never seen before.

Moments later, a trolley rumbled down the street and came to a stop in front of the sign.

The driver leaned forward. "You gotta BOP?"

"We sure do." Mercedes grabbed her mother's hand and pulled her onto the trolley. When she reached the top of the stairs, she pulled a card from her front pocket and handed it to the woman.

"Give it a swipe." The driver pointed to a nearby scanning machine.

"Cool." Mercedes swiped the card and handed it to her mother. "This is yours."

Carlita stared at the card. "What is it?"

"It's a BOP," Mercedes said.

"You got one, too?" The driver asked.

"No. This is a surprise for my Ma. Do you mind if I ride along this one time?"

"Sure. Why not?" The driver pushed the door shut. "Today's our first day, so it's kind of a trial run. Have a seat."

They were the only ones on board, and Carlita and Mercedes sat in the front two seats, directly behind the driver.

Before Carlita could ask Mercedes what was going on, the driver began to speak. "Walton Square and the east side will be my regular route. You can find a schedule online. The trolley will run from seven until nine in the morning for BOP holders and local residents. After that, the regular tourist trolley will run from nine a.m. until six p.m."

The driver explained the new trolley system ran from five in the evening until seven-thirty for the locals who needed a ride home after work.

"Walton Square is now on the new trolley route," Carlita guessed.

"Yep, and I bought you a BOP for the whole year," Mercedes beamed. "You can use it on any trolley at any time. BOP stands for business owner's pass."

The City of Savannah had spent the last year discussing adding a trolley route early in the morning and then later in the evening for both residents and business owners. The goal was to keep cars off the busy downtown streets.

"You won't take my Segway and you don't like to drive downtown," Mercedes said. "This will be the perfect way for you to get around without having to walk everywhere."

"That's so thoughtful, Mercedes. Thank you."

The trolley made a second stop, but no one got on.

"I guess the locals are gonna need some time to buy the passes and get the schedule down," the driver said.

"I bought one of the first passes," Mercedes said. "The cool thing is you can use it for all of the trolleys, both tour trolleys and commuter trolleys."

The trolley pulled away from the curb and Carlita turned her attention to the driver. "Will you be running the locals and tourist trolley in my area?"

"Yep." The woman nodded. "I'll share the early daily route and tourist route with another driver. I'm not sure who that will be. Some of the other drivers are whining and crying about their route. Not me. I'm just happy to have both feet sunny side up." She glanced at Carlita in the rearview mirror. "You own a business in Walton Square?"

"Yes. I own a pawnshop, Savannah Swag, some rental properties and soon, an Italian restaurant, Ravello."

"Nice. I've never worked this side of town. I'm excited to get to know the locals on the east end. My name is Claryce Magillicuddy."

"It's nice to meet you, Claryce. My name is Carlita and this is my daughter, Mercedes."

"I like your accent," Claryce said. "It's rare to hear one of those nasally northerners."

Carlita wasn't sure if she should be offended, but Claryce kept talking and she quickly realized it was nothing personal and more of an offhanded comment. While they rode, Claryce rattled on about her job, how she loved to meet new people.

She'd retired, after working for the city sanitation department as a dispatch operator for decades. "I sat around staring at my four walls for about a month and then I said to myself, 'Claryce, if you sit here staring at these four walls for one more day, you're gonna lose your mind.' That very day, I drove down to the city offices and put in an application for a trolley driver."

"You're retired? You look too young to be retired," Carlita complimented.

"I turned sixty-seven two weeks ago." Claryce patted her hair. "Don't let the luscious spiced cider locks fool you. There's a head full of gray underneath." She glanced at them in the rearview mirror. "You wouldn't happen to know Elvira Cobb, would you? She lives on the east side, somewhere in your area."

Mercedes snorted. "Yes, we...we know Elvira."

"That woman is a royal pain in the rump," Claryce said. "She's always trying to bum a free ride on the trolleys."

"Imagine that," Carlita murmured. "I'm not surprised."

"We had a few words last time she was on my route. She began interrogating a couple of the riders. I warned her to knock it off and she had the nerve to file a complaint against me."

"She's a trip," Carlita said.

The conversation ended when the trolley pulled to the curb and a man wearing a gray business suit stepped on. Claryce showed him how to swipe his card and after choosing a seat behind Carlita and Mercedes, they continued their route.

By the time Claryce and the trolley completed a circle, several more passengers had boarded, getting on and off at various stops. It took a full hour for the trolley to complete the route. By then, Mercedes and Carlita knew Claryce loved living in Savannah, and she loved to gossip.

They waited until the trolley stopped at the corner in front of the pawnshop, before making their way off.

"It was a pleasure to meet you, Carlita and Mercedes. I hope to see you again soon."

"Same here," Carlita said. "Have a nice day, Claryce."

"You betcha. I wouldn't have it any other way." Claryce winked at them before closing the door and driving off.

Carlita watched the trolley until it turned the corner and disappeared from sight. "What an unusual woman."

"She's a character," Mercedes said. "So what do you think?"

"I like her already. She has Elvira pegged."

"No, not that. The BOP? Do you think you'll use it?"

Mother and daughter began making their way back to the apartment. "At first, I wasn't sure, but the more I think about it, I'm sure I'll use it, especially on rainy days when I need to go somewhere." Carlita abruptly stopped. "Thank you, Mercedes. That was so thoughtful."

"You're welcome," Mercedes stifled a yawn. "I'm ready to get home and crawl back in bed."

When they reached the apartment, Mercedes headed to her room while Carlita started a pot of coffee. After pouring a cup of the hot brew, she carried it to the balcony and eased onto a lounge chair.

Rambo followed her out. He placed his chin on the side of the cushion and stared at her.

"Let me guess...you're ready to go for a walk."

Rambo's tail thumped the deck.

"Tell you what - let me finish my coffee and we'll go." Carlita downed the rest of her coffee and set the cup in the sink before meeting her pooch at the door.

The busyness of the day hadn't started and Carlita thoroughly enjoyed their early morning walks. The streets were still quiet and there was a crisp coolness to the air.

When they reached the Waving Girl statue, they paused to greet her before wandering along the walkway to the other end of the touristy riverfront district.

Carlita gave Rambo's leash a gentle tug. "Do you smell that Rambo?" She covered her nose, as the acrid smell of smoke grew stronger with every step. "Something is burning."

Up ahead, she spotted a fire truck and several police cars parked in front of the Mystic Dream riverboat.

Chapter 3

Carlita jogged the rest of the way, joining the outer fringe of a large crowd gathered at the side of the pier. The overpowering smell of smoke hung heavy in the air and she noticed wisps of smoke curling from the rear of the boat.

"C'mon, Rambo." Carlita shifted her pooch's leash to her other hand and made a beeline to the other side for a closer look.

Her eyes shifted up, past a charred rear railing to several firefighters who were inspecting the damage.

Off to one side, she noticed a tall, dark-haired man wearing khakis and a blue polo shirt. He was animatedly waving his arms in the air and Carlita wondered if he was the Mystic Dream's owner, Lawson Bates.

The firefighters stepped out of sight and emerged on the dock, dragging their fire hoses back to the truck. After replacing the hoses, the men climbed into the fire truck and drove off.

Carlita inched past several onlookers in an attempt to eavesdrop on the conversation between the dark-haired man and another man she suspected might be the fire chief. They were still too far away and she only caught an occasional word.

She watched as the second man shook his head. He walked over to a pick-up truck sporting a City of Savannah logo, opened the door and climbed inside while the man Carlita guessed was Lawson Bates, marched off in the opposite direction.

"I guess we better get going." Carlita began to retrace her steps when the sound of screeching tires caught her attention.

A reporter Carlita recognized from a local news channel sprang from the passenger side of a news van. A camera crew was hot on his heels and headed her way.

The young reporter adjusted his earpiece and grabbed a microphone. Carlita took a step back, anxious to steer clear of the camera's line of vision.

"Five, four, three, two..." The cameraman began his countdown and lifted his finger for one.

"Hello, everyone. This is Brock Kensington, Channel Eleven News, reporting live from East River Street in downtown Savannah."

"I'm standing in front of the Mystic Dream riverboat, a Savannah area landmark. City fire crews were called to the scene a short time ago after receiving reports of smoke and fire." Brock motioned behind him. "And as you can see, this iconic Savannah treasure appears to be heavily damaged."

Carlita rolled her eyes. "Heavily damaged?" she muttered under her breath.

"The details are starting to trickle in. From what we can tell, the majority of the damage appears to be located in the rear of the riverboat."

"We're breaking for a brief commercial." Brock began to walk as he talked. "Stay with us, as we hope to have a moment to chat with the owner of the Mystic Dream, Lawson Bates."

The reporter shifted the microphone to his other hand. "For now, reporting from the shores of the Savannah River, I'm Brock Kensington."

Kensington gave a thumbs up and lowered the microphone. "I'll see if I can get closer to Lawson."

"Good luck with that," one of the camera operators chuckled.

"He's a jerk, I know." Kensington straightened his back and smoothed his hair. "Still, it's worth a shot." The reporter made his way toward the man. There was a brief exchange before Kensington glanced at his watch and walked back to join his news crew.

Carlita scooted closer in an attempt to eavesdrop.

"Well?" the cameraman asked.

"Lawson had plenty to say," the reporter said.

"Any finger pointing going on?"

"Yep. All ten of them. You know the drill with Lawson. The man has more enemies than his cousin, Mayor Puckett."

The cameraman shifted the camera to his other shoulder. "Who is Lawson claiming is responsible for the fire?"

"He's insisting it was arson and was throwing out names left and right," Kensington said. "Emmett Pridgen, the chairman of the downtown development committee, who is also trying to get the gambling boat up and running."

"Yeah, he would be the perfect suspect."

"Mark Fox."

Carlita perked up as the reporter rattled off the name of her friend's husband. Mark Fox was a Savannah area property developer. Before she had time to digest that tidbit of information, Kensington rattled off another name...this one making her blood run cold.

"Pirate Pete Taylor. He was the first person Lawson named."

"Pirate Pete is a good guy," the cameraman said. "Why Pete?"

"I dunno." Kensington shrugged. "Lawson was rambling on with all kinds of threats. I hope these guys watch their backs."

The news crew began folding up their equipment and making their way back to the news van.

Carlita hurried after them, hoping to hear more about Lawson's accusations.

"If I can score an interview with those three before the other local stations catch wind of Lawson's suspicions, I might have the story of the season on my hands," Kensington said.

"Excuse me." Carlita tapped on the reporter's shoulder. "I'm sorry to bother you. I watch you on television all of the time and am a fan of your reporting."

The man's expression softened and a slow smile spread across his face. He puffed up his chest. "Thank you. I appreciate the feedback."

"You're welcome. I...I would love to have your autograph, Mr. Kensington, but I don't have anything to write on."

"I'm sure I can find something." Brock reached into his jacket pocket and pulled out a business card. He turned to one of the other news crew. "You got a pen I can borrow?"

The man reluctantly pulled a pen from his pocket and handed it to Kensington.

"What's your name, lovely lady?"

"Carlita." Carlita started to tell him her last name, but thought better of it. "You can just sign it Carlita."

The man signed the back of his business card and handed it to her. "You can catch my next news story at six o'clock. By then, we should have more information about the unfortunate damage to the Mystic Dream."

"So you don't know what happened or how the fire started?"

"Not yet," Kensington replied. "Rest assured that we'll be working nonstop to figure out the cause."

"I'm sure you will." Carlita studied the business card. "Thank you, Mr. Kensington. Keep up the good reporting."

The reporter beamed at her. "It's nice to see my hard work is appreciated."

One of the camera guys snickered and the reporter shot him a dark look.

Carlita thanked him again and then Rambo and she headed back to the edge of the dock where Lawson Bates stood staring at the damage to his ship.

She could see his lips moving, an angry scowl on his face. Lawson's scowl deepened when another man stepped off the riverboat and joined him.

He angrily shook his head and motioned at his damaged ship before marching back on board and disappearing from sight. The second man slowly followed behind.

After they were gone, Carlita pulled her cell phone from her pocket and scrolled through her list of contacts. She tapped out a brief message to Pete, telling him she had some important information and asked if she could stop by to talk to him.

Her second text message was to her friend, Glenda Fox. *Hi, Glenda. It's Carlita. I need to talk to you when you have time. Please call me. It's kind of important.*

She pressed the send button and started to slide the cell phone back into her pocket when it chimed.

Your message sounded urgent. Pirate Pete was the first to reply.

Carlita dialed his number. "I'm down by the river. Someone set fire to the Mystic Dream and Lawson Bates is naming you as one of the possible arsonists."

"You're kidding." Pete paused. "Someone set fire to the Mystic Dream?"

"Yes, and I have more information. I think I should tell you in person. There's a reporter by the name of Brock Kensington who's hot to talk to you about the incident."

"I see." There was another long moment of silence. "I'll be at The Parrot House within half an hour."

"A word of warning, the hotshot reporter may already be camped out on your front step."

"Then I'll take the secret way to work," Pete replied.

"Through the pirate tunnel?" Carlita chuckled.

"Of course. Is there any other way for a pirate to sneak around?"

"I wouldn't know." Carlita promised him she would be there as soon as she dropped Rambo off at home and then told him good-bye.

Her phone chimed again. It was Glenda Fox.

"Hello, Carlita. I just read your message. It sounded important. Is everything okay?"

"I'm fine. I called to warn you and Mark to be on guard." Carlita briefly repeated what she'd told Pirate Pete, that the Mystic Dream was damaged and Lawson Bates was pointing fingers at Glenda's husband.

"Oh dear," Glenda said. "Lawson and Mark have butted heads several times over Savannah area development projects. Lawson seems to think since he's a Savannah business owner and his cousin is the city mayor, he can stick his nose into everything that happens in this town."

"I'm beginning to think I wouldn't like Lawson Bates," Carlita said. "There's also a reporter from Channel Eleven News by the name of Kensington who was on the scene a short time ago. I'm almost certain he's going to try to track down Mark to ask him about the Mystic Dream's fire."

"I know who he is. The man is a pain in the rear," Glenda said bluntly. "Thanks for the heads up. I was going to give you a call to see if you wanted to join me for lunch in the City Market district. I figured I better hit you up before your new restaurant opens and you're too busy for your friends."

"I'm never too busy for friends," Carlita said. "What does your schedule look like?"

"I know it's short notice, but what about this afternoon? There's a new restaurant, getting rave reviews I thought we could check out. It's called the *Garden of Goodness*. The restaurant serves all kinds of baked pasta dishes, wood-fired pizzas, decadent desserts...you name it. Most of it is dining al fresco overlooking some magnificent gardens that were designed by *Southern Style Courtyards*."

"It sounds intriguing. You're making me hungry describing it," Carlita joked.

"Perfect. If three o'clock works, I'll call to see if they take reservations. You can't miss it. It's on City Market's main drag."

"Three o'clock is fine."

When Carlita reached the apartment, she let Rambo inside and stepped into the hall to let Mercedes know she was heading to Pirate Pete's restaurant.

Her daughter's bedroom door was shut and the lights were off. She quickly jotted a note and left it on the kitchen counter before slipping back out of the apartment.

When she reached the Parrot House, Carlita tried the entrance door, and it was locked.

The restaurant didn't open until eleven and it was still too early, so she sent Pirate Pete a text, telling him she was waiting on the front step. Carlita plopped down on the bench to wait.

Why would Lawson Bates accuse Pete of damaging the Mystic Dream? Surely, there was plenty of room for more than one tourist boat on the river.

The sound of a car horn pulled her from her musings. Her heart skipped a beat as she watched the Channel Eleven News van careen around the corner. It was heading her way.

Chapter 4

"Uh-oh!" Carlita dove behind a clump of bushes lining the side of the building and crouched down. She fumbled with the screen of her cell phone and tapped out a quick message to Pirate Pete. *Don't open the door. Channel Eleven News out front.* She pressed send and prayed Pete would check his phone before opening the door.

The news van stopped in front of the entrance. Brock Kensington and the two camera operators exited the vehicle and made their way up the steps.

Carlita held her breath certain that at any moment Pete would open the door expecting to see her. Instead, he would find the news reporter shoving a microphone and a camera in his face.

The seconds ticked by and Carlita's legs started to cramp, but she refused to budge, certain the slightest movement would give her and her hiding spot away.

Brock Kensington rapped sharply on the door. "I don't see a vehicle. Maybe Taylor isn't here."

Numbness spread from Carlita's feet and her knees began to wobble. *Please...hurry up and leave.*

"This is a bust," Kensington grumbled. "We might as well head to Emmett Pridgen's office."

The trio returned to their van and climbed back inside.

As soon as the doors shut and the van rumbled off, Carlita rolled onto her backside and began massaging her calves.

The door to the restaurant slowly opened and Pirate Pete emerged. "Carlita?"

"I'm over here."

"Over where?"

"In your bushes."

The bushes parted and Pirate Pete peered in. "What are you doin' in my bushes?"

"I was hiding from the reporters." Carlita crawled out of her hiding spot. She reached for the wall to steady herself and slowly stood.

"I thought that was my job." Pirate Pete extended a hand. "Let me give you a hand."

Carlita gingerly stepped onto the asphalt. "I sent you the text to tell you I was here. Next thing I know, the nosy news crew was pulling in. I did the first thing I could think of."

"I appreciate the warning." Pete led her inside and closed the door behind them. "I have a feeling I haven't seen the last of them. They'll be back."

"I'm sure they will."

Carlita followed Pete to his office where he motioned her inside before closing the door behind them. "Savannah Fire Chief, Earl

Gillison, called. He's going to stop by this afternoon to 'chat.'"

"Hopefully, Lawson doesn't show up on your doorstep." Carlita pointed at Gunner's empty birdcage. "Gunner isn't here today?"

"He's home. I didn't dare bring him through the tunnels. He gets a little freaked out."

"I don't blame him." Carlita leaned forward in her chair and began massaging her knees.

"I'm sorry you had to hide out in my bushes. I appreciate the heads up." Pete changed the subject. "How did you happen to find out about the fire on board the Mystic Dream?"

"Rambo and I were taking a walk down by the river. When we reached the Mystic Dream, I noticed right away something was wrong."

Carlita told Pete she smelled the smoke first. "When we got closer, I spotted the fire trucks parked in front of the riverboat. From what I could tell, it appears most of the damage was in the back."

"The authorities believe the damage was intentional and not accidental?" Pete asked.

"That's my guess." Carlita's head bobbed up and down. "The roving reporter, Brock Kensington, marched right up to Lawson Bates and asked him. That's how I found out Lawson is accusing you of damaging his riverboat."

"The man has his share of enemies. Any number of people could've been responsible for the damage to the riverboat."

"I heard that, too," Carlita said. "You weren't the only one. He also named Mark Fox and the city development manager as suspects."

Pirate Pete lifted a brow. "Emmett Pridgen?"

"Yes, that was the name." Carlita leaned back in her chair. "Do you think he's naming you because you told him you were opening a pirate ship in Savannah?"

"Could be." Pirate Pete scratched his chin thoughtfully. "He wasn't too keen on the idea, I'll give you that. Thanks again for the warning."

"You're welcome." Carlita glanced at her watch. "I should go. I'm meeting Glenda Fox for a late lunch. I warned her, as well."

"Are you going to warn Emmett Pridgen?"

"No. I heard Kensington tell his crew he wanted to head to Pridgen's office when he found out you weren't going to answer the door."

"Better him than me." Pete stood. "I'll walk you out."

Carlita paused when they reached the parking lot. She squinted her eyes and studied her friend's face. "I haven't had time to review the agreement yet and was wondering about the money."

"We weren't sure how much you were comfortable investing," Pete replied. "We're hoping for at least twenty-five thousand."

61

"I see. Now that I have a dollar figure, it will help me make my decision." During the short walk home, Carlita mulled over the offer. Was she taking on more than she could handle? Three businesses would keep her hopping...a fourth might be too much.

Back at the apartment, Carlita opened the alley door and stepped inside. A loud *thump, thump* echoed from upstairs.

"What in the world?" Carlita climbed to the top of the stairs and placed her hand on the hall wall. The sound was coming from her apartment. She fumbled with the lock and then swung the door open. "Mercedes?"

The music was even louder inside the apartment, so loud that it rattled the doorknob.

Carlita marched down the hall and pounded on her daughter's bedroom door. "Mercedes Garlucci!"

The music continued.

"This is crazy." Carlita backtracked through the apartment and stepped onto the balcony. Rambo was right behind her. "I'll bet the racket is hurting your ears, too." She patted her pooch's head and then dialed her daughter's cell phone number.

"Hello?"

"Mercedes, what is going on?" Carlita yelled into the phone.

"I don't know what you're talking about," her daughter calmly replied.

"The racket! Turn down the racket and meet me on the balcony." Carlita jabbed the *end call* button and began massaging her temples.

"Hi, Carlita."

Cool Bones, Carlita's rear tenant, leaned over his balcony railing and waved. "You having a party?"

"If there's a party, I wasn't invited. I apologize for the racket."

"No worries. When you got a minute, I want to run something by you."

"I'll be over as soon as I figure out what is going on."

Cool Bones chuckled. "Good luck." He stepped back inside and she heard his sliding door close.

The music suddenly stopped and Mercedes joined her mother on the balcony. "What's up?"

"I was going to ask you the same thing." Carlita placed a fisted hand on her hip. "What's up with the disco music? I heard it as soon as I walked into the building."

"I was listening to music." Mercedes shrugged. "Sometimes it helps put me in the writing mood. You weren't home. I figured I wouldn't be bothering anyone."

"Except the neighbors."

"Shelby is at work."

"What about Cool Bones and our new neighbor, Sam Ivey?"

"Oh." Mercedes frowned. "Cool Bones."

"He was out on his balcony, wondering what the racket was."

"Sorry." Mercedes let out a puff of air, blowing her bangs out of her eyes. "I forgot about Cool Bones."

"Because you were too focused on irritating our new tenant," Carlita guessed.

"He started it."

"Started what?"

"He was playing some annoying classical music. It was giving me a headache."

"And yours didn't?" Carlita rolled her eyes. "This nonsense has got to stop. I'm sorry you and our new tenant got off on the wrong foot, but he's here for a year, unless he does something to break the terms of his lease, so you two might as well make peace."

Mercedes crossed her arms and met her mother's hard stare.

"You're stubborn as a mule." Carlita lifted both hands and stared skyward. "I give up."

Mercedes followed her mother into the living room. "I'll run next door and apologize to Cool Bones."

"And Mr. Ivey," her mother added. "Cool Bones asked me to stop by his place. Hopefully, he doesn't want to move out because you're making all of us miserable."

Mother and daughter exited the apartment and made their way to the apartment directly behind theirs. Carlita tapped lightly and the door opened.

Cool Bones opened it wider, motioning the women to come in. "Carlita, Mercedes. How was the disco party?" he teased.

"It's over and I'm sorry," Mercedes apologized.

"It's okay. I figured you was paying me back for all of the times I practice my sax in the apartment."

"Our new tenant, Mr. Ivey, and she have gotten off on the wrong foot and she was paying *him* back for some imaginary offense."

"It wasn't imaginary." Mercedes stomped her foot in frustration.

"He seems like a nice man," Cool Bones replied. "I met him this morning. We exchanged business cards. He's going to recommend the Thirsty Crow to his customers, and I'm going to recommend his walking tours to our patrons."

He patted Mercedes' arm. "Maybe you did get off on the wrong foot. It happens to the best of us."

"How is business?" Carlita asked.

"We got some great gigs lined up, which reminds me. I wanted to talk to you about something."

Chapter 5

"Sure," Carlita said. "What's up?"

"I was thinking about me and the Jazz Boys hosting a little get-together a week from this Friday. I would like to invite the owners of the Thirsty Crow and a dozen or so of the locals who support our business."

"Here at the apartment? It sounds like fun. You know how I love parties." Carlita had already hosted several events since moving to Savannah, one of them a block-party to get to know her Walton Square neighbors. "Do you need help?"

"No, but I was wondering if we could use the courtyard since my apartment is on the small side."

"Absolutely. What time?"

While Carlita and Cool Bones discussed the upcoming party, Mercedes wandered to the window and gazed out.

"It's a shame Ravello won't be up and running before the party." Carlita snapped her fingers. "I could whip up a few of the appetizers I plan to put on the menu, if you want."

Cool Bones patted his stomach. "Carlita, you know that's an offer I can't refuse. You are hands down one of the best Italian cooks in the entire south."

"Flattery will get you everywhere," Carlita joked. "I'll start working on a small sampler menu. In the meantime, I'll let the other tenants know the courtyard will be unavailable not this Friday, but next."

She rattled on as the trio made their way into the hall. "I also have several boxes of twinkle lights from the last courtyard party if you would like to borrow them."

The door to Sam Ivey's apartment opened and the handsome young tenant stepped into the hall. He smiled at Carlita and Cool Bones. When his eyes met Mercedes' eyes, the smile vanished. "Hello, Mrs. Garlucci, Cool Bones." He pointedly ignored Mercedes and focused his attention on Carlita.

"I'm done moving everything into the apartment and finished filling out the apartment checklist you gave me." He handed Carlita a sheet of paper.

Carlita glanced at it. "Thank you. I hope you found everything in working order."

"It is. I'm enjoying the courtyard view. It's been fairly quiet, except for a short time ago when there was some loud music, but it didn't bother me."

"Too bad," Mercedes muttered under her breath, and her mother pinched the back of her arm.

"Ouch!" Mercedes scowled at her mother.

Cool Bones chuckled and winked at Mercedes before turning his attention to his new neighbor. "I was telling Carlita my band, the Jazz Boys, and I would like to host a party down in the courtyard a week from Friday. You're welcome to join us."

"I'll have to check my appointment calendar. If possible, you can count me in. It will give me a chance to meet some of the other neighbors."

"You'll love living in Walton Square." Carlita grasped her daughter's elbow and propelled her forward. "We're glad you're here, Mr. Ivey."

"Sam," the man interrupted. "You can call me Sam."

"Yes. Sam." Carlita cleared her throat. "I'm not one to beat around the bush. I'm going to just speak my mind."

The smile returned to Sam's face. "I appreciate that."

"It appears you and my daughter, Mercedes, may have gotten off on the wrong foot the other day. She seems to think you don't like her."

"I never said that," Mercedes gritted out.

"I don't know where she got that impression," Sam drawled, his eyes slowly shifting to Mercedes. "We did have a slight exchange over her Segway when I was moving in." He tilted his head. "I do apologize, Ms. Garlucci, if I hurt your feelings."

He said it in such a way Mercedes was certain that the last thing he was - was sorry.

Sam Ivey extended a hand. "Shall we start again?"

Mercedes resisted the urge to slap his hand away, fully aware her mother and Cool Bones were watching. Not to mention it would make her appear childish. She hesitantly placed her hand in his and a jolt of heat coursed through her veins.

She quickly jerked her hand back. "Of course."

Sam's eyes twinkled and he slowly slipped his hand into his pocket. "I was wondering about the local cable company, if you could tell me who you use."

Carlita rattled off the name of the cable company and Mercedes excused herself, slipping back inside the apartment and closing the door behind her.

She pressed a hand to her beating chest, surprised by her reaction to Sam Ivey's touch.

She immediately pushed the thought aside, chalking it up to her intense dislike of the man, certain her body was trying to warn her away.

Carlita returned to the apartment a short time later. "Why did you run off? I was hoping you and Mr. Ivey, I mean Sam, could get to know each other better."

"I...didn't have anything to say." It was the truth. As soon as Mercedes touched Sam Ivey's hand, her mind went blank, and she didn't like the feeling one iota. She quickly changed the subject. "What's for lunch?"

"I'm having a late lunch with Glenda Fox. You're welcome to join us."

"Nah. I think I'll call Autumn to see if she wants to run to the shopping mall with me."

"Have you had a chance to look at Pete and Tori's agreement?"

"I gave it a quick glance. It looks like a standard agreement. I didn't see a dollar amount. I gave it to Tony to see what he thinks."

"Thank you."

"I love the pirate idea," Mercedes said. "Maybe we should take another dinner cruise on the Mystic Dream to check it out."

"The Mystic Dream isn't going to be going anywhere anytime soon." Carlita briefly told her daughter about the damage to the boat. She mentioned how she overheard the news reporter

74

say the owner, Lawson Bates, was pointing fingers not only at Pirate Pete, but also at Glenda's husband, Mark. "I called Glenda to give her a heads up and that's when she asked if I could meet her for lunch."

"Maybe you don't want to get involved in this business venture. It sounds as if Bates might be the type to pay Pete back and damage the pirate ship."

"That's a thought, Mercedes. I wonder if Pete thought about that, too."

"I'm gonna give Autumn a call."

"I think I'll take Rambo for a walk."

Mercedes returned to her room while Carlita went in search of her pooch. "You wanna take a quick walk around the block?"

Once outside, Rambo trotted down the alley toward his favorite parking lot watering spot.

While they walked, Carlita thought about the damaged riverboat and Lawson Bates. What if

Lawson convinced himself Pete was the one responsible for the damage and he decided to seek some sort of revenge?

The last thing Carlita needed was to battle a Savannah business owner who had it in for one of her business partners...or even her!

Thankfully, she hadn't committed to Pete or Tori yet. Perhaps it was best if she postponed her decision for a day or two, to see what happened once the pirate ship arrived.

After Rambo watered the grass, they swung by Ravello to inspect the final restaurant renovations.

She found the workers in the back, installing high-end appliances in the commercial grade kitchen. She admired the spacious walk-in cooler, large oven, eight-burner cook top and gleaming stainless steel range hood.

After the brief tour, they exited through the back door and returned to the alley. "What a beautiful day," Carlita told her pooch as she fished her house keys out of her front pocket.

"Help!"

"Did you hear that?" Carlita glanced over her shoulder, but didn't see anything. "My hearing must be going."

She shoved the key in the lock and twisted the knob when she heard a loud clanging noise and a second call for help.

Carlita nudged Rambo inside the apartment.

It was then, she noticed someone dangling from the second story fire escape of the building across the alley.

"Stay here." Carlita slammed the apartment door shut and darted to the back of the building where she found her former tenant clinging to a metal grate. "What in the world?"

"I'm stuck." Elvira's legs swung back and forth. "I need a ladder."

"What are you doing?"

"What does it look like I'm doing? I'm hanging on for dear life," Elvira gasped. "I need a ladder."

"Hold on. I'll see if the restaurant workers have a ladder that will reach you." Carlita ran inside the building and into the kitchen. "I need a tall ladder. Quick!"

One of the workers dropped what he was doing. "There's one in front." He hurried out of the room and returned moments later carrying a large metal ladder.

"I think that will work. Follow me." Carlita led the way out of the building and to what was left of the fire escape. "She's stuck."

"You got that right." The man unfolded the ladder and slid it forward until the top rung was directly below Elvira's feet.

"Hold on." The man slowly climbed the ladder. When he reached the top, he grasped the edge of the metal grate with one hand and Elvira's left leg with his other. "You're going to have to wiggle back a little and then start sliding down. I'll guide you."

Elvira grunted, but did as the man said and slowly inched her way backward.

Carlita shaded her eyes and held her breath as she watched the man guide Elvira to safety. "Whew!"

The man backed down the ladder with Elvira following close behind him.

"Thank you for helping us," Carlita said.

"Yeah." Elvira swiped at her pant legs. "Thanks. You're a real life saver."

Carlita shifted her gaze from Elvira to the fire escape. "What in the world were you doing?"

"I was trying to reach the second story window. I almost cleared the landing when a chunk of it broke off and fell to the ground." Elvira pointed to a section of rusted ladder nearby. "I almost went down with it."

"I need to get back to work." The worker snapped the ladder together and picked it up.

"Wait!" Elvira grabbed his arm. "Do you mind if I borrow the ladder for a few more minutes? I wanna go back up."

"Are you crazy?" Carlita gasped.

Judging by the look on the worker's face, he had the same thought.

"The fire escape is dangerous. What if the other section breaks off and you aren't as lucky this time?" Carlita asked.

"It's a chance I'm willing to take."

"Suit yourself. Bring it back when you're done." The worker returned to the restaurant. When he reached the doorway, he looked back and shook his head before disappearing into the building.

Carlita faced her former tenant. "I thought the upper level of your building was empty."

"It was. I mean it is empty...at least I thought it was until the other night. There's something strange going on over here."

Chapter 6

Elvira unfolded the ladder and adjusted the legs. "I keep hearing funny noises at night and now during the day, so I thought it was time to check it out." She scampered to the top and then gingerly stepped onto what was left of the landing.

"You sure you wanna do this?" Carlita shaded her eyes and gazed up. "What if that thing gives way like the rest of the fire escape?"

"Then I'm going to sue the city. There has to be some sort of safety code about making sure fire escapes are operational and safe." Elvira bounced on the tips of her toes and the fire escape creaked under her weight.

Carlita stumbled backward. "You're crazy."

"Eh. I've been called worse." She swiped her hand across the grimy windowpane and then stuck her forehead against it. "Can't see anything but a bunch of storage boxes."

She grasped the bottom of the sash and gave it a tug. It refused to budge. "I figured this was going to happen."

Carlita rolled her eyes. "It's locked for a reason."

Elvira ignored Carlita's comment as she reached into her pocket and pulled out a small metal tool. She jammed the tool in the windowsill, and began wiggling it back and forth. "It's going to…"

There was a faint popping sound. "Perfect." Elvira slid the tool into her back pocket, lifted the window and stuck her leg inside before turning back. "Call the cops if I'm not out in ten minutes."

She eased through the open window and disappeared from sight.

Carlita stood there for what seemed like forever, listening to muffled banging sounds.

"Elvira" Carlita cupped her hands to her mouth. "What's going on?"

The only answer was another dull banging noise.

"I can't believe I'm doing this." Carlita gingerly stepped on the bottom rung of the ladder. "I should leave her there."

Common sense told her to leave Elvira to her own devices, but Carlita knew she couldn't - not if she thought her former pain-in-the-rear tenant might be injured.

With each rung Carlita climbed, she called Elvira's name.

When she reached the top of the ladder, she leaned forward in an attempt to peer inside the open window. The only thing visible was stacks of storage boxes.

Carlita grabbed hold of the base of the fire escape and wiggled it. Small chunks of rust fell to the ground, but the escape stayed put.

"I must be as cuckoo as she is," Carlita muttered under her breath before she tentatively stepped onto the escape.

It let out a sharp snapping sound. Carlita quickly scrambled across the metal bars and vaulted through the window. In her haste to reach safety, she kicked the ladder. It teetered back and forth before falling over. The ladder made a loud clatter as it hit the ground.

"What was that?" Elvira hurried to the window.

"The ladder. I accidentally knocked it over when I was crawling through the window."

The women peered down at the ladder, lying on its side. "Great. Now how are we going to get out of here?"

"There has to be a stairway leading down to the first floor," Carlita said.

"There is." Elvira motioned Carlita to follow her. The women zigzagged past several stacks of boxes before stepping into a narrow hall. It reminded Carlita of the layout of her own apartment building.

Inside the hall were several doors, all of them closed. "Don't bother trying to get into the other rooms. They're all locked." Elvira pointed to the other end of the hall. "There's the stairs to the lower level."

"Great." Carlita took a step forward.

"You're wasting your time. The exit is sealed off."

Sure enough, there was a wall at the bottom of the stairs.

"I'll give Mercedes a call. She can come over and set the ladder back up."

Elvira followed Carlita to the open window. "Good idea. I would call Dernice, but she's working and I'm the only one home, which is why it seemed like the perfect opportunity to see what was going on around here."

Carlita started to text her daughter and then stopped. "Crud. I just remembered. She's not home. I'll have to try Tony."

She texted her son and he promptly replied he was with a customer and it would be a couple of minutes. She sent a reply, thanking him and then slipped the phone into her pocket. "Did you find anything?"

"Find what?" Elvira asked

"That someone was messing around up here?"

"Oh that. No, but I found some other interesting stuff." Elvira darted to a stack of boxes and dropped to her knees. She flipped the flaps, reached inside and pulled out an old wooden steamer case.

"Check this out." Elvira lifted the lid, removed a large piece of velvet material and handed it to Carlita.

Nestled inside was a gem-encrusted knife. Along with the knife were several old coins.

"These have to be worth some serious cash. Look how old they are."

The first thing Carlita thought of was Pirate Pete and Tori. She ran her thumb over a ruby. "This does look old. I wonder if there are more."

"I was trying to figure that out right before someone vaulted through the open window and then we lost the ladder." Elvira reached for the knife.

"Wait." Carlita tightened her grip on the handle. "Do you mind if I take a picture of it? I want to see if I can figure out its history."

"Sure, but if it's worth anything, it belongs to me," Elvira said. "Finders, keepers…"

"It belongs to the owner of this building, not you."

Elvira held it up to the light while Carlita took several pictures.

"Are there any other treasures inside the box?"

"Nope. That was the only thing. Like I said, I haven't had a chance to go through the rest. I have a hunch this place is a gold mine." Elvira began digging around inside the box while Carlita stood near the window, waiting for Tony to arrive.

Elvira rummaged through several of the boxes. The only things she found were stacks of dated newspapers, some vintage clothing, rusty gardening tools and a stack of tattered paperback books.

Tony appeared in the window. "I would ask you why you're in here, but since this involves Elvira, I don't think I wanna know."

"Thanks, Tony, and you're right," Carlita sighed. "You don't want to know."

Elvira ignored the comments. "I think I'm going to hang around here for a while to see if I can figure out a way to get into the other storage rooms."

"You're on your own," Carlita warned. "I'm leaving with Tony and returning the ladder."

"I won't have a way out," Elvira whined.

"Your choice," Carlita said.

"Fine. I guess I'll go, too."

Carlita watched as Elvira tucked the velvet bag containing the knife and coins under her arm. "That doesn't belong to you."

"I'm borrowing it," Elvira said.

"Whatever." Carlita gingerly stepped onto the fire escape while Tony made his way down the ladder. When he reached the ground, he held the ladder steady. "Is anyone watching the shop?"

"Yeah. Josh just got here. Otherwise, I would've had to close shop to come rescue you."

"I appreciate it, son and I'm sorry to bother you." Carlita hopped onto the ground and they both watched Elvira close the upper window and scamper down the ladder.

"That was fun."

"It depends on who you ask."

"Where'd you get the ladder?" Tony asked.

"I borrowed it from one of the construction guys working at Ravello."

"I'll take it back." Tony carried the ladder to the building across the alley and Carlita turned to Elvira. "What are you going to do with the knife?"

Elvira shifted her feet. "Technically, you're right and it doesn't belong to me. I guess I need to put it back where I found it, but first I want to do a little research."

"I have a friend who might be able to help," Carlita said.

"That'd be great." Elvira turned to go and then turned back. "Thanks, Carlita, for saving my butt."

"You're welcome, Elvira."

Tony joined his mother and they waited for Elvira to return to her apartment.

Carlita slipped her arm through her son's arm and they began walking across the alley. "I've been meaning to talk to you about a family meeting. Tori and Pirate Pete have offered me...offered us a business proposition and I want to go over it before making a decision."

"I'm free tonight. Shelby and Violet are visiting a friend after Shelby gets out of work."

"I'm having a late lunch with Glenda Fox; which reminds me I need to get a move on. What time do you think you can make it?"

"Is seven too late?" Tony asked.

"Sounds good to me. Mercedes should be home by then."

When they reached the hall, Carlita thanked her son again for rescuing them and hurried up the steps. She grabbed her purse off the counter, which was sitting next to the Savannah Trolley BOP Mercedes had purchased for her.

She picked it up and slipped it into the side pocket of her purse. "I guess I should try the trolley." Carlita walked to the corner and gazed up and down the street before consulting her watch. She remembered Claryce telling her that the trolley would be by every hour.

Sure enough, and right on time, the trolley made its way toward her. The door opened and Carlita climbed the steps.

"Hello, Carlita." Claryce gave her a mock salute.

"You remembered my name?" Carlita grinned as she scanned her card.

"Yep. I've got a mind like a steel trap." Claryce tapped the side of her forehead. "Where ya headed?"

"The City Market District."

"Perfect. Have a seat and we'll be on our way."

Unlike the previous ride, the trolley was filled with passengers. Carlita made her way to an empty seat by the window. As she rode, she thought about Pirate Pete and Tori's offer. On the one hand, she wanted to help her friends.

On the other, she would have her hands full once Ravello opened, not to mention Tony and Shelby's upcoming wedding.

She also needed to find tenants for Tony's efficiency and Shelby's two-bedroom apartment.

Perhaps she should let Mercedes become more involved in the rentals. Although Mercedes helped Tony in the pawnshop, they had enough staff to cover most shifts and the pawnshop was Tony's baby.

Of course, Pete and Tori mentioned they were looking for more of a "silent partner," someone who could help with start-up cash. And that was another thing...she needed to figure out the value of the remaining gems.

Tony would be able to give her a ballpark figure, since he dealt with jewels and gems at the pawnshop.

The trolley rolled to a stop near Ellis Square and Carlita made her way off.

"You gonna ride back later?"

"Maybe," Carlita said. "I'm not sure yet."

"Don't forget, the last trolley runs until seven-thirty."

"Thanks, Claryce."

Claryce gave her a thumbs up and waited until a few of the other passengers and she were off the trolley before pulling back onto the street.

City Market was bustling with pedestrians. She could hear the faint echo of music coming from one of the more popular restaurants.

Carlita wasn't sure exactly where the *Garden of Goodness* restaurant was located, so she walked to the end of the main thoroughfare and crossed the street to the other side.

Up ahead, she spotted a familiar figure who began waving. Carlita hurried to Glenda's side and gave her friend a hug. "I hope I'm not late."

"You're right on time." Glenda smiled as she gazed at Carlita's hair.

"What?" Carlita patted her head. "Is something wrong?"

"There appears to be a cobweb clinging to your hair." Glenda tugged on a strand of hair. "I got it."

"Elvira," Carlita muttered.

"Is she still living in the building across the alley?" Glenda asked.

"Yes, and she's as troublesome as if she were still one of my tenants. Maybe even worse now."

The women stepped inside the restaurant. The hostess led them to the spacious open-air courtyard in the back. "Have you dined with us before?"

"Nope." Glenda shook her head. "This is our first time."

The young woman rattled off the daily specials and then told them their server would be right with them.

Carlita's mouth began to water as she studied the lunch menu. "I gotta try the cheesy Italian potpie."

"That sounds good," Glenda said. "You can't go wrong with flaky crusts, melted cheese and chunks of chicken."

The server arrived to take their order. Glenda chose the steak and potato pie while Carlita ordered the Italian potpie.

After the server walked away, Glenda turned to her friend. "Lawson Bates is on the warpath."

Chapter 7

"He's accusing you of sabotaging the Mystic Dream," Carlita guessed.

"Yes. He showed up on our doorstep not long after you called, looking for Mark. Thankfully, Mark is travelling. Actually, he's out of the country in Colombia, South America, but I don't think this is the last we've seen of Lawson."

"You're not the only ones. He accused Pete Taylor and Emmett Pridgen of being involved, too."

"Mark mentioned Pete Taylor obtained a permit to operate a pirate ship for tourism. That would definitely make Lawson angry and Pete a suspect."

"Along with Emmett Pridgen," Carlita said. "Although I'm not sure why Lawson named him."

"But what possible motive would Mark have to damage the Mystic Dream?" Glenda shook her head.

"Does Mark have anything to do with the new development in the riverfront district? Lawson may be looking at it from that angle."

"Yes, he's on the development board. There are a number of other board members. Mark is the main contact for the project."

"Bingo," Carlita said.

"Well, he can accuse away, but he doesn't have an ounce of proof," Glenda said. "I'm going to call Mark after our lunch, to fill him in on what you said. I think we've spent enough time talking about Lawson."

The women discussed upcoming Savannah events including the spring gardens and mansions tour. The tour highlighted a number of the downtown district's award -winning homes and gardens.

"Is your home going to be part of the tour?" Carlita asked.

"Not this year. I decided to take a year off and enjoy the tours instead of working."

The server returned with a tray full of food. She eased Glenda's steak and potato pie in front of her, followed by Carlita's Italian potpie. "Be careful. Both of these dishes are hot."

Carlita picked up her fork and poked a hole in the top of the pie. The fragrant aroma of garlic wafted out and she licked her lips. "This looks delicious."

She scooped out a large spoonful and blew on it to cool it off before taking a small bite. The garlic, mingled with the rich tomato sauce and melted cheese was the perfect combination. "This is delicious," Carlita murmured. "You have to try it."

"And you must try mine."

The women exchanged a spoonful of food, each declaring them a tie. As they ate, they chatted about business, Carlita's children and then Glenda asked Carlita about the cobweb. "What is Elvira up to these days, other than she's giving you cobwebs?"

"She has both her businesses, EC Investigative Services and EC Security Services, up and running. Her sister, Dernice, is living with her and helping out."

"And she's sticking her nose where it doesn't belong?"

"Of course. She claims something strange is going on in the upper level of her apartment building. The owner walled off the stairway, so Elvira decided to climb the fire escape and enter through an upstairs window."

"She's a trip," Glenda chuckled.

"Yes, she is. While she was climbing up, a section of the fire escape broke off. I happened to be walking Rambo and noticed her dangling from what was left of it."

"Good grief."

"So, I got one of the men working at Ravello to rescue her, except she wasn't ready to be rescued."

"She was determined to check it out."

"Of course. When I caught up with her, she was digging around inside a bunch of storage boxes."

"She was trespassing, breaking and entering and then rummaging through someone else's stuff."

"In a nutshell, and depending on whether she returns an item that caught her eye, you can add stealing to the list." Carlita pulled her cell phone from her purse. "She found this in one of the boxes. It was wrapped in a velvet pouch."

She handed her phone to Glenda, who squinted her eyes and studied the screen. "That's an interesting piece. It looks like some sort of antique dagger, but with jewels. You should show it to Pete Taylor."

"I was thinking the same thing."

After finishing their food, the women paid their bills and exited the restaurant. "Would you like to check out the new riverfront project?" Glenda shifted her purse to her other arm. "It's shaping up to be quite a showpiece."

"Is this the one Lawson is ticked off about?" Carlita asked.

"Yes. It's right around the corner and across the street."

"Sure." Carlita patted her stomach. "I could use some exercise after that delicious lunch. I need to bring Mercedes over here."

The women made their way along the cobbled side street and down a steep and curving path.

When they reached the bottom, they veered to the left.

Glenda abruptly stopped in front of a long section of curved marble colonnades. "This is it."

The women's shoes echoed on the gleaming marble tiles as they stepped inside and crossed to the center courtyard. "There's going to be a wonderful mix of businesses in this open-air complex. One end features a small, intimate boutique hotel. The star attraction is the center courtyard, surrounded by unique area shops and artisans. The other end will house a unique mix of eclectic restaurants."

The gentle patter of water splashing filled the courtyard as they circled a multi-tiered and tiled fountain and mosaic pool.

As they walked, Glenda pointed out the various shops. When they reached the other end, they stopped in front of a set of stately stained glass doors. Above the door hung a weathered gray and white oval sign, *Savannah Riverfront*

Inn. Directly below the name and in small letters were the words, *Inquire Within.*

Glenda reached for the knob. The door was locked. "Bummer. I hoped we could peek inside. It's gorgeous."

Carlita followed her friend down the steps and onto the sidewalk. She shaded her eyes and admired the architecture. "This will be a nice addition to Savannah's tourist district."

"I agree." Glenda changed the subject. "I haven't seen the damage to the Mystic Dream. Would you mind circling the block so I can check it out?"

"Not at all." The women fell into step as they walked along the cobblestone streets, passing by several shops and gourmet restaurants before stepping onto the walkway that ran adjacent to the river.

From a distance, it was hard to see the damage to the back of the riverboat. When they got close, the women slowed.

Several men were working on removing a section of charred railing.

"That's terrible," Glenda said. "I can't believe someone would intentionally destroy an iconic Savannah landmark and I can't believe Lawson is accusing my husband."

They walked past the riverboat and started to turn around when something farther along the waterway caught Carlita's attention. It was a ship's towering main mast. "Check it out. I wonder if Pete's ship came in."

Glenda laughed. "Literally."

"I'm serious. He told me it would be here any day." Carlita squinted her eyes. "Sure enough, I think that's Pete's ship."

The women waited for the ship to draw closer.

"It's impressive," Glenda admired the sleek wooden structure. Above the sideboards, was a wide strip of gleaming teak wood featuring fire breathing sea monsters and scowling pirates brandishing swords.

Several crewmembers were working on the upper open deck. "If Lawson was upset before, I can only imagine how he'll react when he sees Pete's pirate ship," Glenda said.

The women continued walking to the other end, where the ferryboat that ran between the Waving Girl Landing and Hutchinson Island was docked, before turning around.

Up ahead, Carlita watched as a group of men marched down the sidewalk and stopped in front of the pirate ship. They hollered out to the workers on deck. Moments later, Pirate Pete and another man joined the men on the sidewalk.

"Uh-oh." Carlita recognized one of them as Lawson Bates. They were too far away to hear what was being said, but judging from the expressions on Lawson and Pete's face, it wasn't a pleasant conversation.

Lawson jabbed his finger at the pirate ship and then pointed at his damaged riverboat.

One of the men stepped between Pirate Pete and Lawson and held up both hands.

"I hope Pete keeps his cool," Glenda said.

Finally, Lawson and his men walked away. Lawson turned back once to say something. This time, Carlita was able to hear him loud and clear. "You're not going to get away with this."

Pirate Pete shook his head, but didn't reply. Instead, the other man and he returned to the pirate ship and disappeared from sight.

"That went well," Glenda commented. "I need to get back to the house. Mark should be calling me soon. I can't wait to tell him about Lawson."

"More like warn him," Carlita said. "And the reporters." She thanked her friend for inviting her to lunch and walked home.

Mercedes hadn't returned from her shopping trip with Autumn, so Carlita settled in at the computer to research some appetizers for Cool Bones' courtyard gathering.

She found several promising recipes, but was having a hard time deciding, knowing part of the decision would depend on whether she could purchase the fresh ingredients in town.

Carlita gave up and then wandered into Mercedes' room. The joint venture agreement was sitting next to her laptop. She picked it up and carried it back to her desk.

The dollar amount was blank, and Carlita remembered Pete throwing out a figure of twenty-five thousand dollars.

Still unable to make heads or tails of the terms, she closed the file folder and wandered into the kitchen to work on dinner when her cell phone chimed. It was Glenda.

"Hello, Glenda."

"Hi, Carlita. I'm sorry to bother you."

"No bother. Is everything all right?"

"I thought I would let you know Fire Chief Earl Gillison was waiting on my porch when I got home. You're never going to guess what Lawson did."

Chapter 8

"Lawson is a busy man," Carlita said.

"He told Fire Chief Gillison he was certain Mark never left town. He claims Mark snuck onto the Mystic Dream sometime during the night and set fire to it."

"That's crazy."

"What a jerk," Glenda fumed. "Mark can prove he is and was out of town. Lawson doesn't have a leg to stand on."

"It sounds like this Lawson has a screw loose. Maybe it was one of his own employees who accidentally damaged the riverboat and won't fess up to it," Carlita theorized.

"Someone needs to warn Pete Taylor. He's probably still down on the river with his new boat. If I were in his shoes, I would leave someone on board the pirate ship to keep an eye on it. I wouldn't put it past Lawson to try something."

"What did Mark say?"

"He's on his way home. He's going straight from the airport to Lawson's place to confront him."

"I'm sorry, Glenda. Let me know if there's anything I can do." After the call ended, Carlita stared at the phone. Did she want to become involved in a business venture already plagued with difficulties?

She wouldn't put it past Lawson to try something, either. If she invested her money, would she have to be concerned about the safety of the ship and crewmembers or potential liability?

Carlita pushed her fears aside and began working on her chicken Milano. She removed a packet of thawed chicken breasts from the refrigerator and began sautéing them in a saucepan.

While she worked, she thought about Vinnie and Brittney. According to Vinnie, he loved being a casino manager. The penthouse apartment was almost finished and he was settling into married life. Her eldest son seemed genuinely happy.

Although Carlita wasn't kidding herself the mafia element wasn't a part of her son's life...after all, Vito Castellini *was* the mob, at least Vinnie wasn't tied to the man's hip, handling all of Castellini's dirty work.

The whole family was looking forward to Shelby and Tony's upcoming wedding, and Carlita secretly hoped it wouldn't be long before Violet became a big sister.

Shelby was tossing around the idea of quitting her job at the post office, but hadn't decided what she wanted to do.

Carlita finished adding the rest of the ingredients and turned the burner on low. She had just finished cleaning up when Mercedes waltzed into the apartment. "Something smells delicious."

"I'm making chicken Milano."

"Yummy. What's the occasion?"

"I invited Tony for dinner. I want to go over Pirate Pete and Tori's business proposal." Carlita wiped her hands on a dishtowel and dropped it on the counter. "I took a look at the agreement again. I can't make heads or tails of it."

"Me either. If you're serious, you might want to contact an attorney."

Carlita followed her daughter to her room. "How is Autumn?"

"Good. She seems to like her new boyfriend, Cole. She wants us to meet him soon." Mercedes plopped down in her desk chair and spun around. "So you gonna let me handle the rental responsibilities after Ravello opens?"

"Gladly, if you're sure you want to take it on." Carlita leaned her hip against the doorframe. "That way, if you don't like the tenant, you have only yourself to blame."

"True." Mercedes reached for her mouse. "If we're not eating dinner 'til seven, I still have a little time to work on my next round of book edits before Tony gets here."

"And I better check on dinner." Carlita wandered back to the kitchen. She wondered what Vinnie, Sr. would have thought of Shelby and Violet...or their son's marriage to the daughter of the head of the mafia.

She wondered if he would approve of her business decisions and what would he say about the pirate ship venture. He would probably think it was crazy.

Carlita tasted the pasta sauce before turning the burner off and sliding the pan to the back of the stove.

"Rambo, would you like to take a walk?" She turned, almost tripping over her pooch who was guarding the stove and keeping an eye out for scraps. His tail thumped on the kitchen floor.

"I'll take that as a yes." Carlita hollered down the hall to let Mercedes know they were going out for a walk.

There was a muffled reply, which she took for an "okay" and exited the apartment. "Let's stop by the pawnshop to remind Tony about dinner."

They waited in the back until Tony finished ringing up a customer's purchase. "We're going for a walk. I stopped by to remind you about dinner."

"How could I forget? My stomach has been reminding me all afternoon."

"I'm making one of my favorites...chicken Milano." Carlita patted her son's arm and headed outdoors, toward the restaurant. The construction workers had finished for the day and the building was quiet and empty.

When they reached John Alder's building, Carlita paused. John and she had gone out a couple of times since the winter masquerade party at Tori's place.

Although Carlita enjoyed John's company, the small spark she'd initially felt had fizzled out. Deep down, she was still grieving the sudden loss of her Vinnie and perhaps even subconsciously comparing John to her deceased husband.

As if on cue, the front door opened and John stepped onto the stoop, almost colliding with Carlita. "I'm sorry, Carlita. I didn't see you standing there."

"It's my fault. Actually, Rambo and I were absentmindedly loitering."

John pulled the front door shut. "I see your dream of opening Ravello is getting closer every day."

"Yes, and I can hardly wait."

"I'm sure it will be a huge success. I promise I'll be one of your first customers."

"That would be nice." Carlita motioned to his building. "When are you opening your bed and breakfast?"

"There's been a change of plans." John paused and cleared his throat. "I'm on my way to Annie's office. I'm putting the place up for sale."

Carlita's heart plummeted. "You're moving?"

"Yes, before the end of summer. I've been offered a consulting job out west, one that's too tempting to turn down." John eyed the side of his building. "I thought coming back to Savannah would be like coming home again, but things have changed." He shrugged. "Or maybe I changed."

"It happens to the best of us." Carlita smiled softly. "We'll miss having you in the neighborhood."

"I'll miss being here. By the time this place sells and I pack up, Ravello will be up and running and you'll barely even notice I'm gone." John said wistfully.

"Perhaps one day you'll change your mind. You'll return to Savannah and things will be different." Carlita was sure he caught her meaning that perhaps things would change between them. Maybe it was wishful thinking. Time marched on and although she was saddened by the unexpected news, she was happy for him.

Carlita impulsively hugged her friend. "No matter where life takes you, please stay in touch."

Rambo began to tug on his leash, his signal he was ready to go. "I better get going." Carlita swallowed the lump in her throat, quickly turned and walked away. She never was good at good-byes.

John's announcement hurt her heart a little, and she wondered if perhaps she cared for him more than she wanted to admit, or more than she dared allow.

Either way, it was probably best. She would be busy running all of her businesses...too busy to spend time and energy on a relationship.

Rambo led the way as they strolled past the *Book Nook*. Carlita caught a glimpse of Tillie, the owner, who was chatting with a shopper near the front window. She gave her a quick wave when she caught her eye.

They passed by *Colby's Corner Store* and then turned back onto their street.

It had been weeks since Carlita had seen Steve Winter, the owner of *Shades of Ink* tattoo shop. Steve was also Autumn's brother. Carlita tugged on Rambo's leash. "Let's stop by and say hello to Steve."

Steve was behind the counter working on his laptop. He glanced up and then did a double take when he saw who it was. "Carlita. I was just thinking about you the other day, wondering when that fabulous new restaurant of yours is going to open."

"Soon. Less than a month. How are you? I haven't seen you around much lately."

"I've been working like crazy." Steve rolled his eyes. "Not to mention, Paisley has been keeping me on my toes."

"Have you finished your upstairs apartment?"

"Yep. We moved in last weekend. You wanna check it out?"

"Sure."

Steve locked the front door of the tattoo shop and then led Carlita to the back. They climbed a narrow set of steps, which opened to a small hall.

Steve's upper level was small, with room for only one apartment. It was modern and sleek and Carlita complimented him on the renovations.

After touring the apartment, they made their way back down. "Autumn told me you rented one of your units to Sam Ivey, a former Savannah cop."

"Yes, and I had no idea he was a cop. He seems so young."

"In his early 30's if I recall correctly. Heard he quit the police force after there was some sort of incident and internal investigation involving him." Steve unlocked the front door of the shop and followed Carlita onto the sidewalk. "It was a few years back and I forget the details. You could probably look it up online. I'm sure the story is still floating around out there in the internet world."

"I might just do that." The two of them chatted for a few more minutes before a customer arrived for his tattoo appointment.

Carlita told Steve good-bye and then made her way back to the apartment. When she reached the hall at the top of the steps, she glanced in the direction of her new tenant's unit.

Curious to find out what had caused the young man to quit the police force and embark on a career of historical walking tours, she headed to her computer as soon as she got inside.

While the computer started, she checked on dinner and then set a loaf of garlic bread on the counter.

She read her emails first, before opening a new search screen. She typed in "Police Officer Sam Ivey Investigation." Several articles popped up. Carlita reached for her reading glasses and slipped them on.

She clicked on the first article. Above the story was a picture of Officer Sam Ivey. Carlita glanced at the caption before scanning the first paragraph. "Oh no."

Chapter 9

According to the story, dated October, 2016, Officer Ivey was in pursuit of a suspect who left the scene of a minor pedestrian accident. The vehicle pursuit started on the edge of downtown Savannah and the main road leading to the highway.

As Sam and the car he was pursuing entered a populated area, close to the highway, Officer Ivey abandoned pursuit, fearing the high-speed chase would end with additional injuries. He turned his siren and flashing lights off and reduced his speed, but the car he was pursuing continued to race down the road.

The suspect failed to navigate a sharp curve and broke through a guardrail, crashing into a large oak tree at a high rate of speed. Officer Ivey was the first to arrive, where a gruesome scene awaited him. It was the body of a young woman, Hailey Silverton. She hadn't been wearing her seatbelt and had been thrown from the vehicle on impact.

An internal investigation ensued and the Savannah Police Department placed Officer Ivey on paid leave. After the investigation ended, he was released back to duty. He submitted his resignation less than a month later.

"How awful," Carlita whispered. She read several more stories, all repeating the same thing and one of them adding that Ivey began offering walking tours in the historic district.

She wandered into the kitchen to turn the oven on and warm the bread. Mercedes emerged from her room and breezed into the kitchen. "What time is Tony coming for dinner?"

"He should be here shortly. I ran into Steve Winter during my walk with Rambo. We got on the subject of our new tenant, Sam Ivey, and the reason he quit the police force. There was some sort of incident and investigation. He couldn't remember the details, so when I got home, I looked it up."

Carlita briefly told her daughter what had happened and her theory Ivey gave up his career because he blamed himself for the young woman's death.

"But he stopped pursuing her. It wasn't his fault she was driving recklessly, not wearing a seatbelt and crashed." Mercedes shifted her feet. "That's what cops do...they chase the bad guys, or in this case the bad girls."

"It does explain a little more."

Tony arrived moments later and Carlita began assembling the food while Mercedes set the table. "We'll eat first and discuss the business proposition later."

The trio gathered at the table where Carlita piled pasta on her plate and then poured a generous amount of sauce on top. She grabbed the bowl of freshly grated parmesan cheese and sprinkled a spoonful on top.

Tony loaded his plate with food and reached for his fork. "This is good stuff, Ma. Something tastes a little different."

"I added a few minced green olives. What do you think?"

"That I'm gonna gain five pounds." Tony patted his stomach.

Mercedes nibbled on a noddle and then dipped it in the sauce. "Ma's pasta is the best. You can eat it with or without sauce, although the sauce is delicious, nice and creamy, just the way I like it."

"The sun-dried tomatoes give it a nice tang." Carlita changed the subject. "How is business at the pawnshop?"

"Good. Now that the weather is warming up, we're getting more foot traffic." Tony rattled off some figures and told them he needed to run a few ads because the store's inventory was starting to dwindle.

They discussed Ravello with Carlita telling her children that Bob Lowman said the last of the punch list was almost completed. "My plan is to start out managing the restaurant. Mercedes offered to help hire the staff. We still have to order food. I've talked with Pirate Pete at length about the restaurant business. He's given me lots of great tips and information."

Carlita tapped the tines of her fork on the edge of her plate. "I wonder if he would be willing to spare his restaurant manager for a day or two to train me on what I need to be doing."

"That's a great idea, Ma. I'm sure he'll help you out," Tony said. "Speaking of Pirate Pete, what are you thinking about his offer?"

"I'm on the fence," Carlita confessed. "On the one hand, I'm always open to making more money. On the other hand, Lawson Bates is making waves, not only accusing Pirate Pete of sabotaging the Mystic Dream but also accusing Mark Fox, Glenda's husband, of the same."

"I've heard the name, Lawson Bates, before," Tony said. "He owns the Mystic Dream?"

"Yes, and it was damaged by fire the other morning."

"What does that have to do with Mark Fox?"

"Mark is in charge of a new riverfront development and I suspect Lawson views it as competition. I dunno if I want to be involved in a project that already has troubles."

"We got enough of our own without any help," Mercedes joked.

"Ain't that the truth."

The trio finished their meal, and it was a joint clean-up effort. As they worked, Tony told his mother and sister that Shelby was starting to work on the wedding plans. The couple decided it would be a small, intimate affair at a chapel not far from Walton Square. All they needed to do was decide on a date.

If they timed it right, Ravello would be up and running. "We can always have a private luncheon at the new restaurant after the ceremony," Carlita said.

"I like the idea. I wanna make sure Vinnie, Brittney, Paulie and Gina can make it since I want my brothers to stand up with me." Tony nodded to his sister. "I think Shelby might ask you to stand up with her, too."

Mercedes' eyes lit. "I would love to be a part of the wedding."

"Don't say nothin'. I think Shelby wants to ask you herself."

"My lips are sealed." Mercedes made a zipping motion across her mouth.

"Now that will be something," Carlita said.

"Mercedes keeping her mouth shut?" Tony joked.

Mercedes whacked her brother's arm. "No! Ma meant having all of the family together again."

The trio returned to the dining room table after they finished cleaning up, and the women waited quietly while Tony set the file folder on the table. "It looks like a standard agreement as far as I can tell, but then I'm no attorney." He tapped the top sheet. "I don't see a dollar amount. The space is blank."

"We noticed that, too," Carlita said. "Pete threw out a figure of twenty-five thousand dollars. I don't know how much money we have left to invest. We still need start-up costs for Ravello."

"I ran some numbers for the rentals and the pawnshop. We're in the green on both fronts. My guess is Ravello will lose a little in the beginning. If we're lucky, we'll break even in four to six months. After that, if we play our cards right, we should be turning a profit."

"I hope you're right," Carlita sighed. "Sometimes I wonder if I've lost my mind, taking on all of these businesses."

"Nah. Those gems have given us the cushion we needed to get going. I did some preliminary numbers on the value of what we've got left." Tony reached into his front pocket and pulled out a folded sheet of paper. "I think it's safe to sell them in the store since the mafia heat is off us these days. If we pawn off what we got left, we would still have around fifty grand to play with, give or take a couple thousand."

"You mean invest in Pete and Tori's venture," Carlita said.

"Yep. I'll leave that up to you."

Carlita gazed at her son thoughtfully before sliding out of her chair. She wandered over to the fireplace mantle and the secret compartment.

"In a way, the gems have been my security blanket." Carlita tugged the pouch of gems from their hiding spot and replaced the mantle before returning to the table.

She untied the bag and shook it lightly, sending the precious gems tumbling across the table.

The emeralds, rubies and diamonds twinkled in the overhead light. Carlita picked up a small diamond and rolled it between her thumb and index finger.

In an odd way, the gems were one of her last remaining connections to Vinnie. That and the Savannah property. Carlita had grown to love her new home. She loved the charm of the city, loved her neighborhood, and had made some genuine friends to boot, something she'd never done in New York, partly because Vinnie didn't want friends. He was more interested in "business associates."

Savannah was in her blood now and as each day passed, New York became more of a distant memory. Day by day, she was putting down roots.

Carlita shifted her gaze from the gems to her children. *They* were putting down roots and making friends...good friends. Pirate Pete was one of them. "I've made my decision. I'll let Pete and Tori know that the most we can invest is twenty-five thousand. It will still leave us an extra cushion."

Tony nodded his approval. "I have the cash on hand in the pawnshop account. You can use it now, and I'll replace it when the gems sell."

Before she could change her mind, she grabbed the business checkbook and wrote out a check to *Pirate Ventures, LLC*, the name listed at the top of the agreement. She signed her name and jotted down the date before placing the papers back into the file folder.

"You gonna deliver the check in the morning?" Mercedes asked.

"No. I think I'll run it over to the Parrot House this evening."

"I'll go with you," Mercedes said. "I could use a little fresh air."

Carlita and Mercedes followed Tony out of the apartment and down the steps. They stopped outside the door to his studio apartment. "You want me to go with you?" Tony asked.

"Nah. I'm sure we'll be fine," Carlita said. "Thanks for helping me figure this one out. I don't want to have too many irons in the fire. I also don't want to pass over a promising business venture."

Tony patted his mother's shoulder. "Pop would be proud of you, Ma. I'm proud of you."

"Thanks, son." Carlita's throat clogged. "It means a lot. I want to make all of my kids proud. I also want to leave something behind for you, including my grandchildren and future grandchildren."

Tony wagged his finger at his mother. "Don't be gettin' any ideas. At least not yet. Shelby and I aren't even married."

"I know. No rush." Carlita thanked her son a second time, and Mercedes and she stepped into the alley.

The evening air was cool and she rubbed the sudden goosebumps on her arms. "I'm already having second thoughts. Maybe I should sleep on it."

"I say we keep going." Mercedes placed a hand on her mother's back and propelled her forward. "You made the right decision. If you're nervous about it, maybe you could change the agreement to twelve months instead of two years."

"But then it would look like I don't trust Tori and Pete," Carlita said.

"It's a business arrangement," Mercedes said. "Don't let your emotions get in the way of making a sound business decision."

"True. I don't wanna be wishy washy," Carlita said. "I'm gonna leave it like it is."

"Good. I think we'll be fine. Plus, it's only twenty-five thousand bucks."

"Only? *Only* twenty-five thousand bucks? That's a lot of money."

"Let me rephrase that." Mercedes linked arms with her mother as they strolled to the end of the block. "At least it's not a hundred grand."

When they reached the Parrot House, the restaurant lobby was standing room only. The hostess told them Pete was out for the evening and wouldn't be back until morning. She offered to leave the file in his office.

Carlita thanked the young woman after handing her the folder and mother and daughter stepped out onto the porch. "You think she'll put it in his office?"

"Yes. You worry too much." Mercedes kept up the conversation during the walk home. She told her mother she was making progress on her new book while her mother teased her about killing off the character who was like their new tenant, Sam Ivey.

"After you told me why he quit the police force, I felt bad for the way I killed him off."

"How did you kill him?"

"Sam was on a solo cave diving excursion. He became trapped in one of the cave's chambers and died when his oxygen tank ran out. It took days before the rescuers recovered his body."

"Mercedes," Carlita chided. "That's terrible."

"What? I was going to have him eaten alive by an alligator."

Back at the apartment, Carlita decided to turn in early. Now that she didn't have to worry about whether to invest in the business venture, she slept soundly and woke to Rambo whining at the bedroom door.

"Ugh!" Carlita glanced at the bedside clock. "I overslept." She grabbed her robe and joined Rambo in the hall.

Her first stop was the kitchen to start a pot of coffee and then they headed outdoors. After a quick trip to Rambo's favorite spot, they darted back inside, nearly colliding with Sam who was on his way out.

"I'm sorry." Carlita took a quick step back and Sam grinned.

"Good morning, Mrs. Garlucci."

"Carlita." Carlita patted her ruffled hair. "Sorry for the bed head look. I overslept."

"You look as fresh as the morning dew," Sam complimented.

"And you look very dapper." Carlita pointed at Sam's striped seersucker suit.

"I'm on my way to meet a group of Tupperware ladies. They booked an early morning walking tour." He placed a tan straw hat on top of his head and gave it a light tap. "I love Savannah this time of the year, don't you?"

"Yes, but then I love Savannah all year-round." Carlita wished Sam a good day and then waited until he stepped out before closing the door behind him. She could hear him whistling as he walked away and she thanked God for giving her a wonderful new tenant, even if Mercedes disagreed.

Back upstairs, Carlita filled Rambo and Grayvie's food dishes and then fixed a bowl of cereal. She poured a cup of coffee and took both onto the balcony to enjoy the cool and quiet morning.

As she ate, she thought about Ravello again. Was she getting in over her head?

It was a little too late to change her mind. The restaurant was almost ready. Would she regret investing in Pete and Tori's new business venture? She needed to make sure they weren't expecting more than a silent partner.

After finishing her cereal, she headed to the computer to check the weather. It was going to be another beautiful day and she began jotting down a list of things she needed to do before Ravello opened.

One of those was to ask Pete if he could spare his restaurant manager for a day or two. She also needed to come up with appetizers for Cool Bones' party.

Carlita turned her computer on and checked her email before beginning her search for recipes. She printed off a handful of promising ones and studied the list of ingredients.

Carlita could hear Mercedes rustling around in her room and glanced at the clock. It was time to call Tori and Pirate Pete to give them the good news. She dialed Pete's cell phone first. The call went right to voice mail, so she tried Tori's number.

Tori picked up right away. "Oh dear. Carlita, I was getting ready to call you."

"I tried calling Pirate Pete. The call went right to voice mail."

"You haven't heard," Tori said.

"Heard what?"

"Someone attacked Lawson Bates last night on the dock near the Mystic Dream."

Chapter 10

"You're kidding." A cold chill ran down Carlita's spine. "Is he going to be okay?"

"He's in the hospital in a coma. The authorities have already stopped by here to ask me a few questions since my name is listed as the second lessee for the pirate ship's docking slip. I assume they've already talked to Pete or are with him now since he's the other lessee listed."

"Because Bates told the authorities, specifically the fire chief, he suspected Pete of setting fire to and damaging his riverboat." Carlita pressed a hand to her chest. "That's awful."

"It is terrible. I left a message asking Pete to call me. I'm sure I'll hear back shortly." Tori changed the subject. "Have you made a decision on partnering up with Pete and me on what may now be our short-lived business venture?"

"Yes. I talked to my children last night. We ran some numbers and as you know, I need to hold onto some of my money for Ravello. We figured we could safely invest twenty-five thousand if that helps."

"It would help immensely. I've got most of my money tied up in stocks right now." Tori breathed a sigh of relief. "Are you sure you want to partner with us now that it appears there will be an investigation? The city may put a hold on our business license until they can sort out this sordid mess with Lawson and his riverboat."

"That might pose a problem, more for you than for me. I guess I should talk to Pete. I know you and Pete didn't damage the Mystic Dream, and I know neither of you injured Lawson."

"The best we can hope for is that Lawson makes a full recovery and can tell the authorities who attacked him." Tori paused. "We had such high hopes for this venture."

"Don't get discouraged," Carlita said. "I'm sure it will all work out."

Carlita thanked Tori for including her in the venture and promised they would talk again soon. She disconnected the call and started to set her cell phone on the counter when she remembered what Glenda told her - how her husband, Mark, planned to confront Lawson when he returned to Savannah the previous evening.

Could it be Mark and Lawson had words, the argument escalated and Mark attacked Lawson? If that were the case, why would the authorities question Tori and Pete?

She quickly dialed Glenda's cell phone. It went to voice mail and then she promptly received a text message from her friend, telling her she would return the call as soon as possible.

Carlita began to pace. It was obvious someone had it in for Lawson Bates. She remembered hearing the reporter, Brock Kensington, saying Lawson also rattled off Emmett Pridgen's name as a suspect in the riverboat damage.

What if Pridgen was behind all of this?

She'd had her first contact with Pridgen when she, along with Elvira and Annie, conducted some undercover surveillance in a downtown club.

Although she didn't know the man, she knew someone else who did...her son, Vinnie. Carlita didn't figure her son would answer her call. She left a message for him, asking him to return the call when he had time.

A sudden thought popped into her head. "That's it." She snapped her fingers. "Hey, Mercedes!"

Mercedes wandered into the living room, her slippers flap-flapping as she traipsed across the wood floor. "Yeah?"

"I thought you were already awake."

"I was earlier. I was up half the night working on my new story and fell asleep at the desk." She began massaging her neck. "I have to stop doing that. It's a real pain in the neck, literally."

"I was gonna tell you I'm heading to the business development office to meet Emmett Pridgen, if he's in."

"What are you gonna do at the business development place? Open another business? Don't we already have enough to do?"

"This is strictly a fishing expedition, for information. Someone attacked Lawson Bates last night. He's in a coma in the hospital and the authorities are questioning Tori, Pirate Pete and Glenda's husband, Mark."

"What does Pridgen have to do with this?" Mercedes started to yawn and covered her mouth. "Sorry."

"When I was down by the river the day the Mystic Dream was damaged, the Channel Eleven News reporter spoke with Lawson Bates. He said he suspected Emmett Pridgen of being one of the people who may have been responsible for the damage to his riverboat."

"Which means he may have also been involved in Lawson's attack. I'll go with you," Mercedes offered. "You'll have to wait for me to get ready."

"I'll wait."

Mercedes ran to the bathroom and Carlita grabbed her phone. She needed to talk to Glenda and Pete before she started snooping around. She poured another cup of coffee and carried her phone to the balcony.

Glenda was the first to call her back. "I can't believe the morning I'm having."

"Let me guess...the cops were on your doorstep, asking Mark if he knows anything about Lawson Bates' attack."

"How did you know?"

"I spoke with Tori Montgomery. They were questioning her, too."

"And Pete Taylor, I suspect."

"I haven't talked to Pete yet, but that's my guess." Carlita sipped her coffee. "Did they tell you what happened?"

"Only that they interviewed the employees, who said Lawson planned to stay late, to keep an eye on the riverboat. A local resident was out jogging along the river early this morning and found Lawson unconscious on the dock in front of the Mystic Dream. The man called 911 and by the time the ambulance got to him, he was in bad shape. They rushed him to the hospital."

"I heard he was in a coma."

"Yep," Glenda confirmed. "That's what the investigators told us. I think Pete may be at the top of the list of suspects."

A wave of dread washed over Carlita. "Why do you say that?"

"Because the investigator, a Detective Polivich, said another riverfront business owner was in the vicinity at the time of the incident."

"Pirate Pete argued with Lawson yesterday. Remember?"

"Yeah, and there were a lot of other people present who witnessed the argument."

"My guess is Pete decided to spend the night on his ship." Carlita set her coffee on the table and wiggled out of the lounge chair. "This is terrible. What makes them suspect Mark?"

"My guess is the comment you overheard the Channel Eleven News guy make, that Lawson suspected Mark, Pete or Emmett Pridgen were behind the damage to his riverboat."

"It's a mess. Until Lawson regains consciousness, we won't know for sure what happened. I would be more concerned for Pete.

It appears he may have been in the wrong place at the wrong time." Carlita thanked Glenda for the information and disconnected the call.

Pete still hadn't called her back. As each minute passed, she grew more concerned the authorities had uncovered evidence pointing to Pete and they arrested him.

Mercedes emerged from the bathroom, comb in hand. "All I have to do is run a quick comb through this mess and I'll be ready to go."

*****

The development office was a nondescript brick building, with a bold, black sign emblazoned on the front door, *Savannah Office of Business Development.*

"Here goes nothing." Carlita grasped the handle and pushed the door open. The interior of the office was as drab as the exterior. Not only was it drab, it was also dark.

Carlita gazed around the room, waiting for her eyes to focus when she spied a small counter off to the side. The young woman behind the counter warily eyed them as they approached.

"Yes. We own a business in Walton Square and have a few questions for Chairman Pridgen." Carlita tapped her fingers on the countertop. "Yes, I believe that's his name...Pridgen."

"Mr. Pridgen doesn't typically handle inquiries in person. We prefer to have them in writing. If you would like to fill out a form." The woman reached under the counter and pulled out a clipboard. "I'll be happy to give it to him."

Mercedes slid in next to her mother. "Do you have any idea how long that will take? We need an answer kinda quick."

The woman smiled patiently. "Forty-eight hours." She pointed to the clipboard. "The development department requires a forty-eight hour turnaround time."

Carlita squinted her eyes at the small print on the top sheet. "The print is too small and I don't have my glasses."

"I'll fill it out," Mercedes said. "Do you know when Mr. Pridgen will be returning to the office?"

The woman glanced at an open appointment book in front of her. "He has a full schedule. He may be back in the office this afternoon, unless his meetings run late. It's hard to tell."

She handed the clipboard and a pen to Mercedes. "Let me know if you have any questions."

The top part of the form was standard information, including name, address and property location.

The lower half was a questionnaire. The questions included the type of business, estimated sales, and estimated customers per day, number of employees they planned to hire and how many of the employees would be related to the owner. The final question was a rough estimate of the percentage the venture would spend on advertising.

Carlita followed Mercedes to a row of chairs on the other side of the room. "I don't remember filling this out for Ravello or the pawnshop," she whispered.

"I don't either," Mercedes whispered back. "Some of this stuff is none of their business. I mean, why should we tell them how many family members we plan to employ? I'm making some crazy business up."

She tapped the pen on top of the clipboard. "I've got it." Mercedes lowered her head and began scribbling.

Carlita leaned over her shoulder and started to chuckle. "That's crazy, Mercedes. Graffiti art studio?"

"It's a real business," Mercedes insisted. "They're big time popular in Europe."

"We're not in Europe. There's no way the Savannah business development members will approve a graffiti art studio."

"It doesn't matter because we don't plan on opening one."

"True."

After finishing the form, Mercedes returned to the counter. The woman glanced at the paper and lifted an eyebrow, but didn't comment on the contents. "I'll be sure to forward your information to Mr. Pridgen. We'll contact you within the next day or so."

Carlita followed her daughter out of the building and onto the sidewalk. "That was a bust."

"Yeah." Mercedes glanced in both directions. "Now what?"

"I'm worried about Pete. He hasn't returned my call. He may be on his pirate ship with poor cell signal. Do you mind if we take a run by there?"

"No. I would love to check out the pirate ship." The women strolled to the corner of the block and crossed the street, making their way to the riverfront district. They passed by the Mystic Dream. The gangway was up and there wasn't a soul in sight.

"I hope Lawson Bates recovers," Carlita said. "Someone must have it in for him."

They continued walking until they reached the pirate ship, anchored only a couple hundred yards away. The gangway was down and the women tentatively stepped onto it. "Hello? Pete? You in here?" Carlita hollered.

The women heard a muffled thump, followed by heavy steps that grew louder.

Pirate Pete appeared, dressed in full pirate garb, from the plumed pirate hat perched atop his head, to his fitted puffy pirate shirt to his shiny black pirate breeches.

"You look like you're ready to conquer the high seas," Carlita teased.

"Or handle a crew mutiny," Pete said. "What brings ya ter my neck of the woods?"

"One, we want to check out your ship," Carlita said. "I left a message on your cell phone earlier."

"You did?" Pete pulled his cell phone from his pocket. "I don't see a call. I've been busy, dodging reporters and defending my territory." His expression grew somber. "Did you hear about Lawson Bates' attack?"

"Yes. I spoke with Tori and Glenda Fox, both of whom were questioned by the authorities. I hope he makes it out of the coma so he can tell them who attacked him."

"Right now, I think they're leaning toward charging me with his attack." Pete went on to explain he was unaware of the incident until the authorities showed up on his doorstep. "The first thing they asked was where I was last night and I told them right here, keeping a close eye on my new ship."

"And they know Lawson claims you may have been responsible for the fire on board the Mystic Dream, as well."

"Tis true," Pete nodded. "I can't believe Polivich questioned Tori. How could a distinguished woman, not to mention a wee bitty thing like Tori, attack a big, brawny man like Lawson? It doesn't make sense."

"I agree," Carlita said.

"Now that you're here, would you like to have a look around?"

"We would love to." Mercedes clasped her hands.

Pete started the tour in the bottom of the pirate ship and the cargo hold, what he explained was the "stores." From there, they climbed up to the crew quarters, located next to the galley, followed by the upper deck. Their last stop was the captain's quarters, the nicest of the areas.

"This is so cool." Mercedes walked over to a hammock hanging from two large wooden posts and gave it a nudge. "Is this where you sleep?"

"Aye." Pete nodded. "Not as comfy as a bed, mind you. Nevertheless, it got me through in a pinch."

Their tour ended on the open top deck.

Carlita wandered to the railing, her eyes drifting to the Mystic Dream. "I'm guessing you didn't see or hear anything last night that might help the authorities figure out who attacked Lawson?"

"Unfortunately, the answer is no. A few of Lawson's employees stopped by this morning to inquire if I was hiring since they're not sure when the Mystic Dream will reopen."

Pete placed his elbows on the railing. "One of Lawson's employees mentioned the investigators took a box out of Lawson's office. He made a comment that he wondered if the authorities would be investigating Lawson now, too."

Carlita perked up. "Investigating Lawson?"

"Yeah." Pete nodded. "When I asked the young man what he meant, he said, 'Lawson might have been involved in some shady business ventures.'"

Pete clenched his jaw and stared at the Mystic Dream. "If only there was a way to sneak on board the Mystic Dream and have a look around."

Mercedes, who joined her mother on the other side, stepped closer. "Where is Lawson's office?"

"It's in the front of the riverboat. Lawson was kind enough to give me a tour before he found out I was bringing my own ship to Savannah." Pete pointed to a long row of windows near the front. "See those windows near the top?"

"Yeah." Mercedes nodded.

"His office is right there."

Mercedes slowly walked across the deck. She leaned over the railing, her eyes focused on the Mystic Dream. "You said the riverboat is temporarily shut down."

"That's what the employees told me," Pete confirmed.

"Perfect," Mercedes said. "I have an idea."

Chapter 11

"I'm not sure about this, Mercedes."

"We'll be fine, Ma. Pete will be our lookout. All Autumn and I have to do is climb the ladder up the side of the Mystic Dream, slip inside Lawson's office, have a quick look around and then sneak back off. It's gonna be a quick and easy in and out, guaranteed."

"I can't believe Pete is going along with this," Carlita said.

"Because it's a simple operation. Plus, Pete's a pirate. That's what pirates do."

"Pirates engage in illegal activities. What if you get caught?"

"Who's gonna catch us? Lawson is in the hospital. Who knows how long it will be before the Mystic Dream is up and running again. Once that happens, our chance to try to figure out what Lawson may have been up to will be over."

Carlita followed her daughter into the living room. "But the authorities already searched Lawson's office. What if you're wasting your time?"

Mercedes shrugged. "Nothing ventured. Nothing gained."

The doorbell rang and Mercedes ran down the steps, returning moments later with Autumn in tow.

"How are you Autumn?" Carlita gave the young woman a warm hug. "I haven't seen you in ages."

"I've been keeping busy at the newspaper. When I'm not working, I spend a lot of my free time with Cole." Autumn grinned, the dimple in her cheek deepening. "Did Mercedes tell you I have a new boyfriend? He's a cop."

"Yes, and now that you mention it; does your cop boyfriend know you're going to break into the Mystic Dream's office?" Carlita asked.

"We're not breaking anything," Autumn said. "Just entering."

"At least we hope we won't break anything. Autumn is kind of a klutz." Mercedes slung her backpack over her shoulder.

"Am not," Autumn pouted.

"I'm kidding." Mercedes squeezed her friend's arm. "We need to get going. Pete is waiting for us."

Autumn stepped into the hall and Mercedes joined her while Carlita trailed behind. When they reached the alley, Carlita caught a glimpse of movement near the tenant parking lot and she watched as Sam Ivey strolled toward them. He was wearing the same seersucker suit Carlita had seen him in early that morning.

"You had a long day," Carlita commented.

"Long and tiring." He tipped his hat to Carlita, ignored Mercedes and turned to Autumn.

"Autumn Winter, this is Sam Ivey, our new tenant."

"Hey, Sam. It's good to see you again," Autumn said.

"Hey, Autumn. I didn't know you knew the Garlucci's."

"I met them the day they moved to Savannah."

"How's Cole?" Sam asked.

The two made small talk and Mercedes and her mother exchanged a quick glance. They needed to get Autumn away from Sam before she slipped and told him what they were up to.

"We should get going." Mercedes tugged on Autumn's arm.

"You're right. Well, it was nice to see you again," Autumn said.

"Tell Cole I said 'Hello.'"

"You coming with us, Ma?" Mercedes asked.

"You go on ahead. I'll be along shortly."

The young women walked away while Carlita and Sam Ivey made their way inside. "Is your daughter always impatient and in a hurry?"

Carlita laughed. "Sometimes. It depends."

They trudged up the steps and paused when they reached the upper hall. "I have something for you. Hang on a sec." Carlita darted into the apartment. She grabbed a plate of cookies she'd baked that morning and carried them into the hall.

"This is my welcome to Walton Square gift." She held out the tray of cookies.

Sam eyed them with interest. "They look delicious."

"It's an old family recipe. The cookies are sugar cookies and the frosting made with cream cheese and lemon zest, my secret ingredients."

"I can't wait to try them. Thank you." Sam took the tray. "Being a bachelor and all, I mainly survive on fast food and frozen dinners."

"I'm sorry to hear that." Carlita almost invited her new tenant to dinner, but changed her mind. Although Mercedes and he had reached a truce of sorts, she didn't dare push her luck. "Ravello will be opening soon. You can come visit as often as you like."

"I will certainly do that." Sam shifted the tray to his other hand. "At the risk of sounding nosy, I was wondering...how many children do you have?"

"Four. My youngest son, Paulie, lives in New York with his wife, Gina. He's the mayor of Clifton Falls, a small town in upstate. My middle son, Tony, runs the pawnshop downstairs. You've already met him."

"He's the one who's engaged to my new neighbor, Shelby."

"Yes." Carlita nodded. "My oldest son, Vinnie, just got married and moved to New Jersey with his new wife. He'll be down for the wedding in a couple of months and, of course, you know Mercedes."

"Yes." Sam solemnly nodded. "Four kids and three businesses. You're a busy lady."

"You betcha. I must like it," Carlita joked. "The kids and the businesses keep me on my toes, especially the kids." She thought of Vinnie's recent marriage to Brittney Castellini, the daughter of the head of the New York mafia and before that, Paulie's temporary split from his wife, Gina.

"I'm sure Mercedes is a handful."

"She has her moments. Most of the time, Mercedes is the least of my worries."

"Thanks again." Sam lifted the tray of cookies. "I'll return the dish when I'm done."

"No hurry," Carlita said. "Have a nice evening."

As Carlita locked the apartment door and headed out to meet up with Pirate Pete and the girls, her own words rang in her ears. Normally, Mercedes was the least worrisome of her children, but not tonight.

*****

The small fishing boat skimmed lightly across the dark waters of the Savannah River.

Mercedes clung to the bench seat, her eyes darting back and forth as they sped away from Pete's pirate ship toward the Mystic Dream.

Pete slowed the engine and they drifted closer, until they were close enough for Mercedes to reach out and touch the side of the boat.

"We'll have to row forward from here." Pete grabbed an oar and maneuvered the small boat along the side of the looming riverboat.

Mercedes spied a small rope ladder dangling from the front quadrant. "We're close," she whispered. "Only a couple more feet."

She leaned to the side, careful to keep her feet evenly planted on the bench seat. Her first attempt to grasp the rope failed. She tried again, delicately lunging forward, mindful of maintaining her balance. Her second try was the charm and her hands tightened around the thick coarse rope.

"I've got it." Holding onto the rope with one hand, Mercedes adjusted her backpack.

Autumn, who was seated on the bench behind Mercedes, tiptoed forward. "You go first."

Mercedes nodded. She sucked in a breath and stuck her foot on the bottom rung.

"We can't be wastin' no time. A freighter could come by anytime and drive us into the side of the boat," Pete warned.

That was all the motivation Mercedes needed. She scrambled up the ladder, and didn't stop until she reached the top. She vaulted over the side, taking a soft roll before springing to her feet.

Mercedes peered down, motioning for Autumn to join her.

Autumn teetered back and forth as she attempted to grab the rope. Her foot slipped on the first try and she flailed wildly, causing the small boat to rock back and forth.

"Hold 'er steady," Pete said.

It was too late. Autumn's left leg went over the side and into the water while the rest of her remained on the boat. "I'm okay! I'm okay."

She quickly pulled herself back into the small boat and crawled to the rope ladder. "I got this." Autumn used both hands to grab the ladder. She darted up the side and didn't look back until she reached the top. "All clear."

Pete fired up the boat's engine. "You remember the signal when you want me to come back to pick you up?"

Mercedes gave him a thumbs up. The women watched as Pete and the small boat slipped out of sight and into the dark night.

"Are you okay?" Mercedes turned to her friend.

"Yeah, just a little wounded pride. My left shoe is a little soggy. I'm fine," Autumn said. "Now what?"

"I studied a diagram of the riverboat's layout. If my calculations are correct, we take these side stairs down one deck and make a left at the bottom. The first door on the left should be Lawson's office."

Mercedes inched forward, her ears tuned to any noises. Although Pete told them that, according to the employees, there was no one on board the boat, the last thing they needed was to be ambushed by a gun-wielding employee who was guarding the vessel.

Squish...squish.

Mercedes abruptly stopped. "Are you making noises?"

"It's my wet shoe." Autumn took a step. "Sorry."

"Let's keep moving."

The stairs creaked loudly with each step they took. Mercedes shifted her feet to the outer edges of the stair treads to quiet the sound.

Autumn, oblivious to the racket they were making, tromped loudly down the stairs.

Mercedes turned back, giving her a warning look.

"What? We're the only ones on board."

"We *hope* we're the only ones on board." There was no time to argue. It was time for action...get in, get out.

Mercedes ran her hand along the wall and let out a sigh of relief when she grasped the handle to what she hoped was Lawson's office door.

She turned the knob, but the door was locked. Mercedes shifted to the side. "Work your magic."

Autumn slid a thin metal pick from her pocket and leaned forward. "It's too dark. I can't see."

"I have a flashlight." Mercedes unclipped a flashlight from the side of her backpack and turned it on.

"Thanks." Autumn grew quiet as she wiggled the lock pick back and forth. Seconds later, there was a faint *pop.*

"Way to go," Mercedes said.

"We're not in yet." Autumn slipped the tool back into her pocket and opened the door.

A blast of stale cigarette smoke greeted them.

"This has to be it." Mercedes waited for Autumn follow her in and then quietly closed the door behind them.

"Now what?"

"We use flashlights to start searching." Mercedes unzipped her backpack and handed Autumn a flashlight. "I want to be out of here in ten minutes tops."

"Me, too." Autumn eased past Mercedes before coming to an abrupt halt. "Was that you?"

"Was what me?"

"Making a thumping noise."

"I don't know what you're talking about."

Thump.

Mercedes stopped dead in her tracks. "I do now!"

Chapter 12

Mercedes slowly lifted her eyes, gazing fearfully at the wooden beams overhead. The seconds ticked by, but she didn't hear the thumping noise again. "I think we're paranoid. Let's get moving."

"I'll take a look inside the desk drawers." Autumn opened the top desk drawer and began sifting through the contents while Mercedes crept over to the filing cabinet in the corner.

She opened the cabinet and shined her flashlight inside. "Who puts boxes of snack crackers in their filing cabinet?"

"Me. I keep snacks in my office desk all of the time," Autumn said. "But I keep the drawer locked. You'd be surprised at how many people think it's perfectly fine to help themselves."

The second drawer down was filled with an assortment of tools and hardware. The third was more of the same. The bottom cabinet was empty.

Mercedes eased the bottom drawer shut and stood. "That was a bust. You got anything?"

"Yeah. It looks like the Mystic Dream business files are in this drawer." Autumn shined the flashlight onto the desk as she scanned the top file. "This looks like employee files. There are a bunch of names and dates. Probably wouldn't be a bad idea to take a picture of this." She pulled her cell phone from her jacket pocket, switched it on and snapped a picture.

"There's another sheet, too. Wow! It looks like Lawson has gone through a bunch of employees in the last several months. He must be a real jerk." Autumn snapped another picture and then closed the file before placing it back inside the drawer.

While Autumn continued her search, Mercedes tiptoed to the other side of the room to a set of bookcases. "I see several interesting books about Savannah's history. I would love to check some of these out at the library."

Mercedes finished scanning the bookshelf before making her way along the perimeter of the compact office, past a porthole, a small coffee station and finally an empty coat rack.

Nearby, a large ship wheel clock ticked loudly, a reminder they needed to move fast.

"I'm almost done," Autumn muttered.

"I'll check the files on top of Lawson's desk." Mercedes sifted through the folders including menu planners, kitchen food inventory and a profit and loss statement. She paused when she reached a folder containing bank statements.

"Jackpot!"

"You found something?" Autumn dropped the folder she was holding.

"Well, for Ma I did. This is a copy of the Mystic Dream's profit and loss statement, menu planners and food inventory. These might come in handy for Ravello." Mercedes whipped her phone out of her jacket pocket and began snapping pictures.

"I'm done. If there are clues here, I'm missing something." Autumn shoved the file folder in the drawer and pushed it shut. "What's behind door number one?" She pointed to a wooden door not far from the hall door.

Mercedes joined her friend. "You first."

"Uh-uh." Autumn stepped to the side and motioned to Mercedes. "You first. I insist."

Mercedes twisted the knob and gingerly opened the door. She tightened her grip on her flashlight as she peered around the corner. Inside the small room was a toilet and pedestal sink. It reeked of mildew mingled with urine. "Gross."

She clamped her hand over her mouth and quickly scanned the room before slamming the door shut. "It's a nasty bathroom."

"Shhh." Autumn pressed her finger to her lips. "You're going to wake the dead."

"Did you hear that?" Mercedes lowered her voice.

"What?"

"That." The faint sound of wailing sirens grew louder. "We need to get out of here."

Mercedes followed Autumn into the hall, pulling the door shut behind her. "Lead the way."

With a quick glance behind her, Mercedes followed her friend up the steps. She was almost to the top when her foot slipped. She reached for the railing, but it was too late.

Mercedes teetered for a moment before falling backwards and tumbling down the steps.

Chapter 13

"Oh my gosh!" Autumn raced down the steps and dropped to her knees. "Mercedes, are you okay?"

"I...think so." Mercedes pushed herself to a sitting position and rubbed the back of her head. "Klutzy me missed a step."

Autumn helped her friend to her feet. "I probably dripped water on the steps and you slipped on it."

The women carefully made their way back up the steps.

"Are you sure you're okay?" Autumn fretted.

"I'm fine." Mercedes stepped onto the open deck where a droplet of rain splashed her cheek. A low rumble of thunder followed. "We better get out of here before a storm lets loose and Pete can't come back for us."

The women stayed low as they made their way to the rope ladder.

"I'll signal Pete." Autumn placed her fingers in her mouth and belted out two sharp whistles.

"I think I see him." Mercedes pointed to a shadow near the stern of the ship.

"I'll go first." Autumn scampered down the ladder, just as Pete and the small boat eased alongside the Mystic Dream.

Once Autumn was safely on board, Mercedes began to back down the ladder. She was eye level with the deck when a movement near the steps caught her eye. She could've sworn she saw someone dart to the other side.

She paused for a moment to see if she could spot the person again and then mentally shook her head, certain her eyes were playing tricks on her.

When she reached the bottom of the ladder, she hopped off the last rung and landed lightly in the bottom of the boat.

A flash of lightning lit the sky, followed by another rumble of thunder, this one closer than the last.

"Hang on, ladies. We gotta get a move on if we want to beat the storm." Pirate Pete hit the gas and the small fishing boat skimmed over the open water.

The light mist turned into a steady shower. By the time they reached Pirate Pete's ship, the skies were lit up like the Fourth of July.

Pete tossed the rope to Carlita, who was standing near the water's edge waiting for them. She quickly secured the small boat and then helped her daughter and Autumn make their way onto the dock. Pete was the last to join them and they raced down the sidewalk.

The pirate ship gangway was open. They darted inside, seconds before the skies opened up and sheets of rain pelted the sidewalk.

"That was a close one." Pete and the women stepped away from the gangway. "I was beginning to think I would have to leave you girls on the riverboat until the storm passed."

"Well?" Carlita asked. "Did you find anything in Lawson's office?"

"Sure did," Mercedes said. "I found Mystic Dream's profit and loss statement, their menu planners and food inventory worksheet. I figured the information would come in handy for Ravello."

"Did you find anything that might be a clue as to who set fire to the Mystic Dream or attacked Lawson?" Pete asked.

"No," Autumn said. "The office was clean."

"At one point, right after we got there, we could've sworn we heard someone above us on the open deck," Mercedes said. "Then, when we were leaving, just before I started down the rope ladder, I thought I saw someone near the staircase."

"Was it a man or woman?" Pete asked.

"It was too dark to tell, plus I only caught a glimpse out of the corner of my eye," Mercedes said. "It could've been my mind working overtime."

"So you found nothing at all?" Pete pressed.

"Some employee lists," Autumn shook her head. "No wonder Lawson's employees are looking for another job. He goes through employees like I mow through bags of potato chips. I took pictures of the employee logs and Mercedes snapped a few pictures of the restaurant end of things. Would you like to see what we've got?"

"Yes, if you could forward a copy. Perhaps I'll pick up on something," Pete said.

"I would like a copy, too, since I wouldn't mind taking a look at how the Mystic Dream runs its restaurant operations." Carlita turned to Pete. "Which reminds me, I was wondering if you could spare your restaurant manager for a couple of days around the time I open Ravello?"

"Of course," Pete said. "I appreciate Mercedes and Autumn taking a quick look around Lawson's office for me, although I think I should have gone along."

"Who would have manned the getaway boat?" Mercedes pointed out. "Ma couldn't do it. I would've tried, but then you might not get your boat back in the same condition. I have a hard enough time driving a car during daylight hours."

"Ditto here," Autumn agreed. "Besides, we're always up for a little sleuthing, especially for a worthy cause. Just don't mention it to Cole. He would give me an earful."

"Cole is Autumn's boyfriend," Carlita explained. "He's also a police officer."

"Speaking of police officer," Pete said. "How is it going with your new tenant, Sam Ivey?"

"Good," Carlita said.

"He's a pain in the rear," Mercedes said.

"Mercedes," Carlita shook her head.

"Okay. He *was* a pain in the rear. I'm withholding my final opinion." Mercedes changed the subject. "Now what? We're back to square one and not any closer to figuring out what's going on with Lawson and his riverboat."

"I was thinking about it while I was pacing the sidewalk, waiting for you to come back," Carlita said. "Glenda Fox's husband, Mark, met with Lawson last night to confront him about his accusations. I wondered if maybe Lawson said something that might be a clue, so I called Glenda while I was waiting. We're going to stop by her place after we leave here."

Carlita turned to Pete. "Before I go, my old tenant, Elvira Cobb, found something in a box in the apartment building where she lives. I took a picture of it and wondered if this was something you might recognize."

She scrolled through her phone and pulled up the picture of the coins and gem encrusted knife Elvira found before handing her phone to Pete.

"You said your former tenant found these?"

"Yes. They were buried in the bottom of a storage box."

Pete tapped the screen to enlarge the picture. "It's not uncommon to find valuables in historic Savannah homes or even buried in the backyards of Civil War era homes. Rumor has it Savannah has millions of dollars in buried treasure. Prior to the arrival of Sherman's troops, the citizens of Savannah buried their valuables. When the city fell into ruin, the majority of the treasures simply could not be relocated because the owners fled or abandoned their properties."

"Or died," Carlita said.

"Yes - or died," Pete nodded.

Mercedes perked up. "Does that mean there may be treasures buried on our property?"

Pete chuckled. "You mean even more than you already found in the basement?"

Carlita shot him a quick look, hoping the comment passed over Autumn's head. Unfortunately, it did not.

"You found buried treasure in your basement?" Autumn gasped. "You never told me that."

"It was a lucky find," Carlita mumbled. "I'm sure it won't happen again. Let's not mention this to Elvira. She'll be digging up the parking lot, the courtyard, you name it."

"True," Mercedes laughed. "We better not give her any ideas."

"I'll tell her what you said Pete, but then I'm sure she's going to break into the upstairs again and tear the place apart."

"Does the landlord know?" Pete asked.

"No. She snuck in through an upstairs window." Carlita sighed. "It's a long story."

The heavy rain turned to light sprinkles and she shifted her gaze out the gangway door. "The storm is letting up. We should get going if we want to stop by Glenda's place before it gets too late."

Pete accompanied them off the ship. "Thanks again for taking a look around the Mystic Dream. I owe you one."

Carlita cast a wary glance up and down the sidewalk. "Be careful tonight, Pete. I worry Lawson's attacker isn't finished and might be after you, too."

"I got my trusty dagger handy."

Autumn's eyes grew wide. "You have an honest to goodness pirate dagger?"

"No," Pete laughed. "I was kidding, but I do have a loaded Colt pistol. Would you like me to walk you to your car?"

"No. I think we'll be all right." Carlita eyed the side of the pirate ship. "With all the talk of Lawson's attack, I haven't thought to ask you when you think the pirate ship might be up and running."

"Now that my good friend and partner has given me some much-needed working capital, I'll start interviewing employees tomorrow. I figure within two weeks we'll be christening this beauty." Pete admired the side of his ship. "I've got a few names I'm kicking around."

"We can't wait to hear what you come up with."

It was a short drive to Glenda's house. The front porch lights were blazing brightly and Carlita eased the car into an empty parking spot directly in front of the house. "Don't say anything about sneaking on board the Mystic Dream."

"Mum's the word." Mercedes patted her mouth.

Carlita climbed the front steps and waited for the girls to join her before pressing the buzzer. The door slowly opened and Glenda's butler, Reginald, peered down at them. "Yes?"

"Hello, Reginald. Carlita Garlucci. Glenda is expecting me...expecting us."

Reginald opened the door wider and motioned them inside. "Follow me." His heels clicked sharply on the gleaming floor as he escorted the women down the long hall, to the back of the house.

He stopped abruptly in front of a door Carlita knew opened to the library. He knocked twice before opening the door and stepping to the side.

Glenda sat facing the fire while her husband, Mark, was seated across from her. She sprang from the chair. "Carlita. I almost forgot you were stopping by."

The first thing Carlita noticed was the pale and pinched expression on her friend's face. "Let Reginald take your wet jackets." Glenda's hand shook as she motioned to Reginald.

Carlita waited for the butler to exit the room before turning to her friend, a concerned expression on her face. "Are you okay? You're pale as a ghost."

"The authorities left here not long ago. They claim to have found some information in Lawson's office."

Chapter 14

"I'm guessing it wasn't good."

"It was a log of dates, if you will, where Lawson claims Mark was harassing him, trying to shut down the Mystic Dream and destroy his business."

"Where did he come up with that crazy notion?" Carlita asked.

"I have no idea. There was also another name the detective mentioned, one I didn't recognize." Glenda turned to her husband, a blank expression on her face. "Do you remember the name, Mark?"

"It was Kyle Flinch," Mark said.

"Flinch...Flinch." Carlita repeated the name. "Why does that name sound familiar?"

Mercedes tapped her mother's arm. "TG Flinch. Remember her? She owns *The Ghost Roast. The Ghost Roast* is the site of the Madison Square murders."

"Ah." Carlita lifted a brow. "She was the goth girl. She scared the you-know-what out of me when we met her. Sweet gal, though. I wonder if she's related to this Kyle Flinch."

"It's not a common name," Glenda said. "The investigator asked a bunch of questions about the downtown building project, how well Mark and Lawson knew each other and the last time he saw Lawson."

Carlita interrupted. "You mentioned yesterday that Mark planned to confront Lawson about his accusations."

Glenda turned, giving her husband an anxious glance. "Yes. Mark did and unfortunately, it wasn't a pleasant exchange."

"Were there witnesses?" Carlita asked.

"Yes." Mark slowly rose from the chair and limped across the room. "I accused Lawson of being a bully and informed him he didn't own the City of Savannah. He told me he would have his cousin, the mayor, shut down my project. I got a little hot under the collar. I told him he'd better not do that or he would be sorry. One of Lawson's employees was there during our entire conversation."

"We suspect the authorities are working on a search warrant," Glenda said. "I would warn Pete if I were you."

"The authorities have already talked to Pete." Carlita went on to explain Pete was concerned after having his own confrontation with Lawson, and spent the previous night on board the pirate ship, expecting Lawson to try something.

"Let me guess...Pete was there alone at the time of Lawson's attack and he has no alibi," Mark said.

"Yes, so it looks like both of you are in the same boat," Carlita grinned. "In the same boat, get it?"

Glenda briefly closed her eyes. "Unfortunately, yes."

"I'm sorry. That wasn't funny." Carlita patted her friend's arm. "Let's hope Lawson comes out of his coma and can tell the authorities who attacked him."

The five of them chatted for several more minutes and then Carlita told them they needed to get going. She thanked the couple for letting them stop by to ask questions and then the trio followed Reginald to the front.

Carlita waited until they were on the steps and Reginald closed the door behind them. "What do you think? Do you think Mark Fox struck Lawson?"

"I don't know Mark," Mercedes said. "If truth be told, we don't know Glenda that well, either. Lawson sounds like a real jerk and has his share of enemies. Either Mark has horribly bad luck or he was involved in the attack."

"I can't imagine Mark Fox attacking Lawson," Autumn said. "He doesn't strike me as the violent type."

Carlita and the girls made their way down the steps. "What about Kyle Flinch? That's the first I heard his name."

"We ought to check it out." Mercedes slipped into the passenger seat and reached for the seatbelt. "He might be able to shed some light on Lawson."

A sudden thought popped into Carlita's head and she tightened her grip on the steering wheel. "What if the authorities put a hold on Pete's pirate ship license?"

"Or they revoke the license," Mercedes said. "We'll be out a cool twenty-five k."

"We can't let that happen," Carlita vowed. "We know Pete didn't attack Lawson. We have to figure out who did and I think we move on to the next logical person."

"Kyle Finch?"

"Him and Pridgen." Carlita glanced at the clock on the dash. "I bet *The Ghost Roast* is still open. I'm hungry for a snack. You up for it?"

"You're driving." Mercedes settled into her seat. "Maybe we'll see a ghost while we're there."

"I would love to go with you, but I need to get home." Autumn glanced at her watch. "Cole is meeting me at the apartment."

After dropping Autumn off, Carlita headed to the restaurant. Although it was well past the dinner hour, they were still busy.

"I see a table for two." Mercedes and Carlita zigzagged past several tables until they reached a small table near the back. It offered a clear view of the front of the restaurant and a partial view of the kitchen.

"I wonder if TG is here," Carlita said. "Do you remember her real name?"

"Tierney Grant. Tierney Grant aka 'The Ghost,' remember?"

"Yeah. Catchy for sure." A male server approached and handed them each a menu. "Welcome to *The Ghost Roast*. Can I get you something to drink?"

"Water will be fine." Carlita glanced at the man's nametag, *Jim*. "We're wondering if TG, I mean Tierney is around."

"She's in the back. Would you like to see her?"

"If she has time. She may not remember us. Tell her it's Carlita and Mercedes Garlucci. She gave us a ghost tour a coupla months ago."

"Sure thing. I'll be back in a minute to take your order."

The women perused the appetizer section of the menu. "Jalapeno poppers sound good," Mercedes said.

"Uh-uh." Carlita patted her stomach. "I'll be up all night."

"Mozzarella cheese sticks with marinara sauce?"

"I think I can handle those."

The server returned a short time later with Tierney trailing behind, a wide smile on her face. "Mrs. Garlucci, Mercedes. It's nice to see you again. Have you opened your restaurant yet?"

Carlita smiled back. "You have a good memory, Tierney."

"It goes with the territory. Are you here to munch or pick my brain?"

"Both," Mercedes said. "We'll take an order of the mozzarella sticks with an extra marinara sauce."

"Good choice. Tierney's marinara sauce is the best." The server jotted the order on his notepad and walked away.

"Do you have a minute to join us?" Mercedes asked.

"Sure." Tierney dragged a chair from the empty table next to them and plopped down. "How's business on your side of town?"

"We haven't opened Ravello yet. We're close, though. That's not the reason we're here," Carlita said.

"Oh?" Tierney lifted a brow.

"Have you ever heard the name Lawson Bates?"

"Bully Bates?" Tierney asked.

Carlita lifted a brow. "I take it you're not a fan, then."

"Not at all. He's a ruthless business owner."

"Lawson's riverboat, the Mystic Dream, was damaged a couple of days ago. Last night, someone attacked him and he's in the hospital in a coma," Mercedes said.

"We have friends who are also business associates and are suspects in both the attack and the fire," Carlita added.

"Someone finally went after Lawson. I'm surprised it took this long."

"The reason we're here is the authorities mentioned another name...Kyle Flinch. It's not a common name and we wondered if you knew Kyle."

"Are you serious?" Tierney's mouth fell open. "Kyle is my brother. He works for me, but before that he worked for Lawson on the Mystic Dream."

"Then consider this a courtesy visit and your warning the authorities will soon be talking to Kyle about Lawson's attack."

"They can talk away," Tierney said. "Kyle was here all last night, until closing. After closing, we went back upstairs to our apartment. Kyle is staying with me until he can afford a place of his own."

"You were with him all night?" Mercedes quietly asked. "I'm sure the authorities are going to ask the same thing."

"Well, I mean, he was in the apartment all night."

"Would it be okay if we asked Kyle a couple of questions?" Carlita asked. "Maybe he can shed some light on why Lawson would name him."

"Sure. He's in the back cooking. I'll go get him." Tierney popped out of the chair. She returned a few minutes later, carrying their plate of mozzarella sticks and accompanied by a young man who looked a lot like Tierney.

"Kyle, this is Mrs. Garlucci and her daughter, Mercedes." Tierney slid the plate of food onto the table. "They want to ask you a couple of quick questions about Lawson Bates."

The young man eyed them warily as he swiped his bangs from his eyes. "Okay."

"I need to head back to the kitchen." She patted her brother's shoulder and smiled at Carlita and Mercedes before walking away.

"We'll make this quick. I know you're busy. How well do you know Lawson Bates?" Carlita asked.

"I worked with him for about six months. I started out in the kitchen prepping. By the time I finished, I was a server. Lawson liked to 'cross train' his employees. One week you worked in one spot. Another week you worked somewhere else."

"Did you like working for Lawson?" Mercedes asked.

"In the beginning he was all right. After a couple of months, he started acting weird."

"Weird like how?"

"Like secretive. He kept hiring and firing people. As far as I know, he never gave anyone a raise. In fact, he kept threatening to cut our wages. By then, *The Ghost Roast* was getting busy and Tierney needed help anyway, so I quit."

Mercedes reached for a mozzarella stick. "I wonder why he would name you as one of the suspects who may have set fire to the Mystic Dream."

Kyle shrugged. "We got into an argument and I walked out. I told him one of these days he was going to tick off the wrong employee and they wouldn't put up with his crap."

"And he remembered that?" Mercedes dipped her stick in the sauce and took a big bite. "I betcha there was more than a coupla employees who had it in for Lawson."

"That's a fact. I was working on a petition before I left, demanding my three-month review. I even told him I was going to contact the labor board."

"You mentioned Lawson was acting secretive," Carlita said. "Secretive as in how?"

"For starters, he would never let any of us close the restaurant. He always insisted on being the last one out. One night, a couple of weeks before I quit, I decided to hide out to see if I could figure out what he was up to and why he would never let anyone close with him."

Kyle explained he clocked out and walked off the ship. He waited nearby for the rest of his co-workers to leave and then snuck back on board before Lawson locked up.

"He didn't see you sneak back on?" Carlita asked.

"No. There's a set of side stairs that lead up to the main deck area where Lawson's office is located. Not many employees know about them. I found them by accident. I saw Lawson heading down to lock up, so I knew the coast was clear. I snuck into the storage closet next to Lawson's office. There's a gap in the door and I figured I could see what was going on if Lawson returned. I stayed in there for a long time. I almost gave up, but didn't because Lawson left the lights on. I knew he would at least come back to shut them off."

"Did Lawson return to his office?"

"Yep." Kyle nodded. "He wasn't alone. He was with another man."

"Could you hear what they were saying?"

"I could hear them talking. Actually, it sounded like they were arguing."

Carlita shifted in her chair. "What were they arguing about?"

"I wish I knew."

Chapter 15

"I thought you said you heard them." Carlita shook her head, confused.

"Oh, I heard them all right and if I spoke Spanish, I would've been able to understand what they were saying. All I know is from the tone of the conversation, it wasn't a friendly one."

Kyle explained Lawson and the stranger went into Lawson's office and shut the door. He stayed inside the closet for another hour before the men emerged. "Lawson shut off all of the lights and I hung out inside the closet a little longer until I was certain the coast was clear."

"How did you get out?" Mercedes asked, remembering how Autumn and she used the rope ladder hanging off the side of the ship to make their getaway.

"I couldn't leave through the main entrance. I would've tripped the door alarm. Instead, I made my way down to one of the lower decks. There's a window inside the galley that doesn't latch. I snuck out through the window."

"It's a shame you didn't know what they were saying," Mercedes said.

"I do know a couple of words. Dinero for money and recoger. They said recoger a few times, so I looked it up," Kyle said. "It means pick up."

"They were talking about money and pick up. Maybe the man was one of the food vendors," Carlita theorized.

The server interrupted when he returned to the table to ask if they needed anything else.

"That's about it." Kyle abruptly stood. "I better get back to work. I'm sorry I wasn't able to help."

"You did help." Carlita thanked him for his time and watched Kyle walk away before turning to her daughter. "What do you make of it?"

"It's hard to tell. It could be something, or it could be nothing. The fact the man showed up after hours is interesting...maybe." Mercedes reached for another mozzarella stick. "This marinara sauce is delicious. I'm trying to figure out what makes it so tasty."

Carlita reached for a cheese stick, dipped it in the sauce and bit the end. "The garlic gives it a nice flavor. Maybe we should serve these as appetizers at Ravello."

"It would be a huge hit." Mercedes polished off the rest of her food. "I wonder if Tierney would mind sharing the recipe."

Tierney dropped by their table while they were gathering their things and Mercedes complimented her on the sauce.

"Thanks. It was my grandmother's recipe and a restaurant favorite. Would you like a copy?"

"We would love the recipe." Mercedes rattled off her cell phone number and Tierney jotted it down on her notepad. "I can't wait to visit Ravello after you open."

"Now that you have our number, we should keep in touch." Carlita said.

"It's always nice to have someone else in the restaurant business to bounce ideas off," Tierney said.

"I agree." Carlita smiled. "Thanks again for bringing Kyle out to talk to us."

Tierney walked them to the door. "I hope the authorities are able to figure out who attacked Lawson."

Mercedes thanked Tierney again. She stepped onto the sidewalk and held the door for her mother. "I wonder if one of Lawson's employees attacked him. I wish we could track some of them down."

"I got a few thoughts on that." Carlita climbed into the car. "The fact Lawson's property was damaged while no one was around, his attack was at night and Kyle confirmed Lawson was doing business dealings after hours are all clues. We gotta figure out how they all tie in together."

"Motive and opportunity," Mercedes said. "Unfortunately, there seems to be ample motive and opportunity for Pete and Mark Fox."

"Then there's Emmett Pridgen," Carlita pointed out.

When they got back to the house, Carlita went straight to the computer, anxious to pore over the photos Mercedes and Autumn had taken inside Lawson's office. She not only wanted to look for clues, but also see how Lawson ran his restaurant operations.

She scrutinized the menu planner first, before examining the kitchen inventory. The last thing she studied was the Mystic Dream's profit and loss statement. She scanned the list and paused when she reached the labor column.

No wonder Kyle and the other employees threatened to file a petition. Lawson's labor costs were low, and although Carlita wasn't in the restaurant business quite yet, she remembered reading the rule of thumb for restaurant wages was twenty to thirty percent of gross revenue, except for certain workers.

Lawson's statement showed his employees' salary and wages at fifteen percent. She studied the other items on the statement, which included inventory, depreciation, marketing and utilities. Her head began to swim from all of the figures and she leaned back in her chair.

Perhaps Carlita was getting in over her head. Her vision of creating mouthwatering Italian dishes for hungry patrons was looking more like a side job, and the tedious paperwork and pencil-pushing turning into her main responsibility. She closed her eyes.

"Ma! Are you okay?"

Carlita bolted to an upright position and clutched her chest. "Mercedes, you are gonna give me a heart attack!"

"I'm sorry. I didn't mean to scare you. I thought you heard me."

"With my eyes closed and my head back?" Carlita shifted in her chair. "Is everything okay?"

"Yeah. I was thinking about what Kyle Flinch said and then you mentioned you had an idea."

"Since I'm officially a partner *and* we're opening our own restaurant, I was going to ask Pete if I could sit in on his job interviews. He mentioned that some of the Mystic Dream employees already stopped by, asking about jobs. I figured we might be able to question Lawson's employees on what they think happened to their boss."

"I was thinking the same thing," Mercedes said. "It would be the perfect opportunity to get a feel for the job market and maybe figure out what was going on after hours on board the Mystic Dream."

"I'll ask him right now." Carlita texted Pete to ask him about cross interviewing and then waited for him to reply.

Her phone began to ring and she picked it up, expecting it to be Pete, but it was Tori.

"Hi, Tori."

"Hello, Carlita. I'm sorry to bother you. I just got off the phone with Pete. The city development department and specifically Emmett Pridgen, have put a hold on our business license pending an investigation."

"On hold?" Carlita began to feel lightheaded. "What was the reason?"

"Because of the police investigation into Lawson Bates' attack. Apparently, the authorities searched Lawson's office and came up with some sort of evidence implicating Pete."

"And Mark Fox."

"Yes. And Mark Fox." Tori muttered under her breath.

"I'm sorry, I missed what you said."

"I heard Pridgen was being investigated, too. His name was on Lawson's list. I think he's trying to cover up his own involvement. The man is a snake."

"You think crooked Pridgen was somehow involved in Lawson's attack and he's trying to deflect the blame onto either Pete or Mark Fox?"

"That would be my guess." Tori sighed heavily. "I heard about your daughter and Autumn's sleuthing mission and it was a bust."

"Not entirely." Carlita glanced at her computer screen and the Mystic Dream's profit and loss statement. "I got some good information on restaurant management. I am curious as to why Lawson's labor expenses are so low. Mercedes and I managed to track down one of Lawson's former employees. He gave us an inside scoop and we're still trying to figure out what it means."

"We need all the help we can get. This business venture could remain in limbo for months, even years. If Lawson doesn't recover, Pete could be facing even more serious problems than never getting this pirate ship business off the ground."

"Along with Mark Fox, not to mention Kyle Flinch. We'll keep working on it on our end." Carlita thanked Tori for the call and then disconnected the call.

Mercedes watched her mother set her cell phone on the desk. "I guess that means we don't have to interview potential employees for the pirate ship jobs."

"No. It means we need to get on it ASAP. Time is money. If Pridgen is involved in Lawson's attack, the last thing he'll want is for us to be snooping around. My guess is he'll try to pin this on someone else. We need to get to Lawson's employees before they find employment elsewhere and slip through our fingers."

Carlita decided it was time to call Pirate Pete. When he answered, she couldn't help but notice the tense tone of his voice.

"We'll get this all sorted out," Carlita promised. "I want to begin by interviewing some of Lawson's employees."

She almost mentioned Kyle Flinch, how he suspected Lawson was up to something when he snuck back on board the Mystic Dream, but decided to keep the information to herself.

"Have you started interviewing for positions at Ravello?" Pete asked.

"Not yet. I figured I could kill two birds with one stone...look for clues on who attacked Lawson and maybe see if there are any potential employees for Ravello as well as the pirate ship.

Speaking of the pirate ship, you still have to pick out a name. The Pirate Ship won't do."

"I've been mulling over names for a while now. I want somethin' people won't forget," Pete said. "But there's no sense in wasting my time on picking a name, at least not right now."

"You won't be wasting your time," Carlita said firmly. "We will get to the bottom of this. You said you already spoke with several of Lawson's employees. Did you happen to get any of their names?"

"Yes. A couple of them filled out applications." Carlita could hear papers rustling in the background. "One of the employees is Luke Markham. He left his number. I'll give him a call to see if he knows of any other co-workers we can contact."

"Good. You work on that. Let me know when you'd like me to run by to help with the interviews."

After the call ended, Mercedes headed to her room, claiming she wanted to do a little background research on Pete, Mark Fox, Emmett Pridgen and the Mystic Dream.

Carlita turned in early, worn out from the long day. Despite her exhaustion, visions of a cool twenty-five thousand dollars going out the window kept her awake most of the night.

She woke early the next morning and started a pot of coffee. Grayvie, Carlita's cat, joined her in the kitchen and began rubbing against her ankles.

She reached down to pat his head and scratch his ears. "We've got ourselves a real sad situation, Grayvie. We need to figure out who attacked Lawson Bates and get our pirate ship out on the waters."

Carlita picked him up and held him close. She absentmindedly wandered to the balcony door and gazed out.

A flash of light caught her eye, and she watched as Elvira flitted past a second story window. "She didn't." Carlita set Grayvie on the floor and stepped onto the balcony.

Sure enough, Elvira was in the upper level of the building across the alley. She wasn't alone. Carlita caught a glimpse of Dernice, Elvira's sister, as she marched past the window. "I hope the owner catches them."

Their movement was non-stop as they hurried back and forth. Carlita remembered what Pete said about the Civil War era treasures.

Perhaps she didn't want to tell Elvira what Pete said, certain her former tenant would start digging holes all over the courtyard, the alley and the properties, in search of more treasures.

Carlita made her way to the balcony railing and leaned over the edge, waiting for another Elvira sighting. When she saw Elvira pause in front of the window, she cupped her hands to her lips. "Elvira!"

Elvira stuck her head out the window. "What?"

Instead of answering, Carlita wagged her finger at her as she shook her head.

Elvira promptly closed the window and disappeared from sight. "If I had her landlord's name, I might have half a mind to call him to let him know what she's doing."

A breathless Mercedes burst onto the balcony. "I was up half the night doing some research on Pirate Pete, Emmett Pridgen and Mark Fox, and you'll never guess what I found out."

Chapter 16

"Let me back up," Mercedes said. "I got to thinking about Mark Fox; you know how Glenda told you he was away on business in Colombia?"

"Right." Carlita nodded. "That's why there's no way Mark set the Mystic Dream on fire. He was out of the country."

"True, but in Colombia." Mercedes stared at her mother expectantly.

"I'm not following."

"Colombia, South America. They speak Spanish."

Carlita's eyes widened. "Which is what Kyle said Lawson and the stranger were doing - speaking Spanish."

"If you went to Colombia on a business trip and the native language was Spanish, don't you think you would need to speak Spanish, too?"

"Oh no." Carlita began to pace. "Perhaps Lawson and Mark were in the middle of a business deal, something went south and Lawson and Mark fought."

"But why wouldn't Mark confess to arguing with Lawson?" Mercedes asked. "It seems out of character for him."

"If Mark attacked Lawson and he recovers, he could easily name Mark as the one who caused his injuries," Carlita said. "He's a well-respected businessman in this area."

"Who has a lot of business connections as well," Mercedes pointed out. "I also picked up on our visit with Glenda and Mark that they both seemed kind of uncomfortable and did you notice Mark limped when he crossed the room?"

"No, I didn't notice. I must be losing my touch," Carlita said. "Now what do we do?"

"Obviously, we can't prove Mark and Lawson became involved in a physical altercation. It sounds as if the authorities are already investigating," Mercedes said. "I have a little more digging around to do, but thought I would tell you what I came up with so far."

Restless, Carlita ran down to the pawnshop, which had just opened, to see if Tony needed any help. She chatted with her son and then headed out the front door.

Carlita cast a glance at the large *Riverfront Real Estate* sign propped up in the window of John Alder's place, something she hadn't noticed before. She crossed the street, stopping briefly in front of the window and then continued walking toward Annie's real estate office.

She could see Annie sitting at her desk, her head down.

Carlita quietly eased the door open. The overhead door chimed and Annie looked up.

She smiled when she saw Carlita. "Hello, Carlita. What brings you to my neck of the woods?"

"I'm mulling over a mystery. Do you have a minute so I can bend your ear?"

"For you...I have two." Annie motioned to an empty chair. "I'm sure you heard John Alder is selling his place and moving away. I was surprised when he asked me to list his property. You two were getting close."

"There was a small spark between us. I have to admit it turned into more of a friendship." Carlita sank into an empty chair. "I guess I'm not ready for romance. Maybe I'll never be ready."

"I know the feeling. There are days when I get a little lonely and it would be nice to have someone to do things with, but other times, especially when I talk to friends who are in the midst of marital drama, I'm glad I'm single."

"Drama...that's the last thing I need," Carlita said. "Have you had any interest in John's place?"

"There's been a great deal of interest. I predict he'll have multiple offers in the next day or so. Commercial real estate is a hot commodity in Savannah. Businesses are looking to come to the area. The fact John already did the legwork and obtained a business license makes the property even more appealing."

"Speaking of business licenses, I signed on a business venture with Pirate Pete and Tori Montgomery."

"You mean the pirate ship over on the river?" Annie adjusted the bridge of her glasses. "Everyone is talking about it. Well, that and Lawson Bates' attack."

"Yep. I invested some of my money and now the city development department has put the license on hold because Pete Taylor is under investigation."

"That's awful. I know Pete and I know Lawson. Lawson is a hard man. Even so, I can't imagine Pete jeopardizing his business reputation to settle a score with Lawson."

"I agree." Carlita shifted in her chair. "Before Lawson's attack, right after someone sabotaged the Mystic Dream; he was pointing fingers not only at Pete, but also at Mark Fox and Emmett Pridgen."

"Emmett Pridgen is another story. The man should not be in city politics. Remember the deal with the Black Stallion illegal gambling mess?"

"How could I forget? I don't trust Pridgen, either. I think he's crooked."

Carlita laid out her theory of what happened to Lawson that it was an inside job and one of his employees or perhaps Emmett Pridgen was involved in the attack.

She told Annie about Mercedes and her conversation with Kyle Flinch, how Lawson was meeting someone in his office after hours, how he didn't know what was being said because they were speaking in Spanish. "He said he knew two words...dinero for money and recoger meaning to pick up."

"If we can't get this mess sorted out and Pete's pirate ship sailing on the high seas, there's a chance I'll have to kiss my cash good-bye."

Ping. Carlita glanced at her phone. "Speak of the devil."

She motioned to Annie and pressed the answer button. "Hi, Pete. I was just thinking about you."

"Hello, Carlita. I'm sorry to bother you this early. I have some good news and some bad news."

Chapter 17

"I'll take the good news first."

"I've actually got two bits of good news and one bad. With the help of Luke Markham, I lined up several interviews for first thing tomorrow morning. Lawson's employees are anxious to get to work. Fair or not, I didn't mention we might not be opening soon."

"Don't worry," Carlita said. "I'm looking for restaurant employees. What's the other good news?"

"Lawson is starting to come out of his coma."

"That's great news."

"The bad news is so far he can't remember what happened the night of his attack."

"Maybe his memory will slowly come back."

"I hope so," Pete said. "If you want to join me here tomorrow around nine, I have half a dozen interviews lined up."

"Perfect. I'll be there." Carlita thanked him again, promised she would meet him at the ship around nine the next morning and then disconnected the call.

Annie waited until the call ended. "You think the employees may be able to shed some light on Lawson's activities and perhaps figure out who attacked him and damaged the Mystic Dream?"

"That's the plan. The only clue is Kyle Flinch overhearing Lawson talking to a man in Spanish, not to mention the low wages Lawson was paying his workers. I saw them for myself. Lawson is ripping his people off."

"Lawson showed you his books?" Annie asked.

"Not...quite." Carlita fidgeted in her chair. "Mercedes kind of stumbled upon them during a recent fact-finding mission."

Annie laughed. "Let me guess. Mercedes broke into Lawson's office."

"Breaking might be the wrong word." Carlita's eyes met Annie's eyes. "Who am I kidding? Yes, Autumn and she broke into his office." She hurried on. "With the Mystic Dream shut down, it was the perfect opportunity."

"Too perfect to pass up?" Annie lifted a hand. "The less I know the better." The office phone began to ring. "I need to take this call. I'm waiting on another real estate agent who wants to show John's property."

"I'll let you get back to work." Carlita gave Annie a wave and headed to the door.

On her way home, Carlita decided to stop by the restaurant. The door was open, so she wandered to the back where the pungent smell of fresh paint filled the room.

She cleared her throat when she spotted a worker perched on the top step of the ladder.

"Mrs. Garlucci." The worker climbed down. "We are almost done with the kitchen."

"It looks fabulous," Carlita said. "I'm almost ready to start ordering small appliances."

The man smiled widely. "It will be a nice restaurant. I can't wait to bring my wife here. I tell her every day how nice this place is going to be."

"Thank you, Gary. I can't wait for it to open, either."

Gary led her around the room, showing her the work they'd completed the previous day. After admiring the changes, she stepped into the alley.

She was almost home when she noticed the back door to Elvira's apartment was ajar. Carlita nudged the door with the tip of her shoe and stuck her head inside. "Elvira?"

Carlita could hear rustling sounds coming from the other room. "Elvira?"

Elvira appeared. "Hey, Carlita. What's up?"

"Does your landlord know you and your sister have been upstairs snooping around, maybe even stealing?"

"Not stealing. Borrowing is a better word." Elvira shrugged. "Besides. He doesn't care."

"I find that hard to believe."

"What are you...the landlord patrol?"

"Of course not." Carlita pointed at a cardboard box next to the door. "Is that a box from upstairs?"

"Maybe." Elvira stepped in front of the box. "How's your new tenant, Sam Ivey?"

"He's fine. He's a nice man."

"I thought you didn't want cops living in your building," Elvira said.

"What is that supposed to mean?"

Elvira examined her fingernails. "Sketchy past, sketchy present, sketchy family."

"I do not have a sketchy past, present or family," Carlita fumed. "That's absurd."

"Is it?" Elvira lifted a brow. "Far be it from me to judge others."

"How kind," Carlita briefly closed her eyes. "This conversation is going nowhere. I'm sorry I stopped by."

"I didn't mean anything by the comment." Elvira followed her into the alley. "We all have skeletons in our closets, although yours might be a little more colorful. You aren't going to tell Davis I was upstairs looking around, are you?"

Carlita snapped her fingers. "Davis. I couldn't remember your landlord's name. Thanks for reminding me."

Elvira stomped her foot. "Crud. I knew I shoulda just shut up."

"I'm not going to contact Davis, but you should be mindful of what you do. One of these days you're going to get into real trouble."

"No risk, no reward." Elvira shrugged. "I'm willing to take my chances."

Carlita shook her head as Elvira slipped inside her apartment and closed the door behind her. "One of these days, Elvira. One of these days."

The rest of the day passed uneventfully with Mercedes holed up in her room working on her book. She emerged around lunchtime to grab a bite to eat and then went right back to work.

Later that afternoon, Shelby and Violet stopped by to drop off some flowers Violet insisted they pick for Nana.

Carlita's heart melted at the little girl's thoughtful gift. "I love them Violet. Thank you so much." She knelt down to give her a gentle hug. "I ran into Beebs the other day. He asked when you and I were going to visit him and Miss Tori."

"I drew a picture for Beebs. We're going to swim in Miss Tori's swimming pool."

"I think it will be too chilly for a February swim. We might have to wait until the water warms up."

Carlita stood. "Let me get with Tori to see what day works for her and Beebs."

Shelby smoothed her daughter's hair. "Violet includes Beebs in her nightly prayers and asks God for him not to be sad anymore."

Sudden tears burned the back of Carlita's eyes as she thought of how Byron/Beebs lost his young granddaughter, Lilly, a couple of years back. According to Tori, Violet reminded him of her.

"I shall get with Tori in the next day or so to plan a visit," Carlita promised.

After Violet and Shelby left, Carlita wandered to the computer and sank into the chair. She started sorting through her emails when her cell phone began to ring.

It was Carlita's son, Vinnie.

"Hey, Ma."

"Hey, son. How are you?"

Vinnie cleared his throat. "I'm fine."

Carlita's heart skipped a beat, immediately sensing something was wrong. "You don't sound fine. Son, what is it?"

"It's about Brittney."

Chapter 18

"We're going to have a baby."

Carlita said the first thing that popped into her head. "Already? I mean you just got married. I thought you would spend some time getting to know each other first."

"It wasn't planned." Vinnie paused. "I thought you would be excited."

"I am. I mean. Yes, of course, Son. You'll make a wonderful father." Carlita shifted the phone to her other ear. "A lot has changed for you in the last few months. Marrying Brittney, moving to New Jersey, starting a new job and now a baby."

"Ain't it great?" Vinnie said. "Things are lookin' up for Vinnie Garlucci."

"Yes, they are. I'm happy for you...happy for Brittney." Carlita swallowed hard and forced the next words out. "Happy for the Castellini family."

"Thanks, Ma. I already told Paulie and Tony the good news. I'll let you tell Mercedes." Vinnie rattled on about his new job; how he loved living in New Jersey and that it was a great place to raise a family.

They chatted about Tony and Shelby's upcoming wedding. Carlita questioned him about Emmett Pridgen, and Vinnie claimed he only met him once. Finally, he told his mother he needed to get back to work.

"I love you, Son. Congratulations again. You'll be a wonderful father." She told her eldest son good-bye and then sat staring blankly at the phone.

Mercedes waltzed into the dining room. "Who were you talking to?"

"Vinnie. He called to tell me Brittney is pregnant."

"What? A baby already? They just got married."

"I said the same thing. He seems excited."

"Wow. Better him than me."

Carlita gave her daughter a pointed stare. "You don't even have a boyfriend."

"See? Like I said, better him than me." Mercedes glanced at the clock. "It's getting late and I'm getting hungry."

"I haven't thought about dinner." Carlita suggested pizza and Mercedes easily agreed. After placing the order, the women wandered into the living room to wait.

"I couldn't find anything else on Mark Fox, Emmett Pridgen or Pirate Pete." Mercedes reached for the television remote. "Pete's only link to Lawson is the pirate ship and the fact he was guarding his ship the night of Lawson's attack."

"With what you said earlier, I'm beginning to think Mark Fox argued with Lawson. Glenda even told me beforehand that Mark planned to confront Lawson the night of his attack. Add in Mark's mysterious limp, plus the fact Kyle Flinch said Lawson was secretly meeting with someone who spoke Spanish."

Carlita continued. "I was certain it was one of Lawson's employees. There's still the damage to the Mystic Dream. Glenda insists Mark was out of town when the damage occurred."

"Maybe Mark had someone do the dirty work for him, knowing he had an ironclad alibi," Mercedes suggested.

"I hadn't considered that angle. We're still missing something. Maybe I shouldn't meet Pete in the morning to interview potential employees."

"I say you go to cover all of the bases. Plus, we're going to need workers for Ravello soon." Mercedes flipped through the channels as Carlita mulled over the possible suspects. She started to say something else when the outer bell rang. "Our pizza is here. I'll go down and get it."

She hurried out of the apartment and down the steps before peering out the peephole. She swung the door open and motioned the delivery person into the hall. "Pizza for Garlucci?"

"Yes, ma'am."

"I already paid for the pizza and breadsticks and left a tip online."

"Yes. Thank you. I need you to sign the receipt." The man handed her a pen and a slip of paper.

After signing, she handed it back and pointed at the pizza boxes. "I only ordered one pizza plus an order of garlic knots."

The man frowned as he studied the receipt. "I have you down for two large pizzas - a meat lover's pizza and another with ham, onion and mushrooms, plus an order of garlic knots."

"Are you sure?"

"Yep." The man held out the boxes of food. "This is your lucky day. Two for the price of one."

She watched the delivery man disappear into the alley before climbing the steps. Carlita balanced the pizzas on her hip and reached for the doorknob when Sam Ivey's apartment door opened and he stepped into the hall.

"Hey, Sam."

The top pizza box began to slide. Sam lunged forward and grabbed it.

Carlita smiled gratefully. "Thank you, Sam. You always seem to be in the right place at the right time."

"It's a gift," Sam joked. He eyed the pizzas and sniffed appreciatively. "Monster Pizza. I would recognize those boxes and smells anywhere."

"They have the best pizza in all of Savannah. I only ordered one, but there was some sort of mix-up and they gave me two." She gave her new tenant a quick glance. "Mercedes and I won't be able to eat two large pizzas. Would you care to join us for dinner?"

Sam started to shake his head. "I don't want to impose."

"I insist. We have plenty of pizza."

"Are you sure?"

"Positive." Carlita nodded her head firmly. "We would love the company."

At least Carlita would love to have Sam to join them. Mercedes might be another story.

She pushed the front door open, and Sam followed her inside. "Look who's joining us for dinner?"

"I...you." Mercedes glared at her mother.

Carlita ignored the look. "The timing was perfect. Monster Pizza accidentally gave us two pizzas instead of one. I ran into Sam in the hall while I was struggling to bring the food inside, so I invited him to dinner."

"How thoughtful." Mercedes forced a smile and hurried to the kitchen.

"Have a seat at the table, Sam." Carlita took the pizza box from her tenant. "Would you like water or tea? I don't have any sodas."

"I've got a liter of Coke in my fridge. I'll go grab it." Sam disappeared into the hall.

Mercedes waited until he was gone. "Why did you invite him to dinner?" she hissed.

"Why not? We have extra pizza. He looks hungry." Carlita placed the pizza boxes in the center of the dining room table. "I thought you two were gonna start over and you were gonna give him a chance."

"I am. That doesn't mean I'm thrilled about him being in our house, sitting at our table and me being forced into polite inane conversation."

"Then we'll let him do the talking. He has a fascinating job. I'm sure he knows all about Savannah's history, which I, for one, can't wait to hear."

Sam returned to the apartment and carried the large bottle of Coke to the kitchen. "I'll pour the drinks."

Carlita directed him to the cups and the ice in the freezer.

"I feel like I owe you for the pizza."

"Mercedes and I were just saying you must have some fascinating stories on Savannah's history. Maybe you can entertain us with a story or two."

"Of course." Sam finished pouring the drinks and carried them to the table.

"We also ordered the garlic knots with the special dipping sauce." Mercedes removed the lids on the sauce. "You know what, Ma? Tierney never sent me her grandma's marinara recipe."

"Tierney Grant?" Sam asked.

"Yeah. We were over there sampling some of The Ghost Roast's appetizers. Tierney has an amazing marinara sauce," Mercedes said.

"They have delicious grinder sandwiches I highly recommend." Sam waited for Mercedes and Carlita to have a seat before sitting down. "Thanks again for inviting me for pizza. I was on my way out to grab a bite to eat."

"You must get lonely living alone," Carlita said.

"My job keeps me busy." Sam shrugged. "I'm perfectly content by myself."

The trio loaded their plates with slices of pizza and buttery garlic knots.

Sam took a big bite of pizza. "It's been awhile since I've eaten Monster Pizza. This is delicious."

Mercedes remained silent while Carlita and Sam chatted about life in Savannah and living in Walton Square. They discussed the upcoming tourist season and how Sam worked twelve-hour days during the height of the season.

"Holidays are busy, too. St. Patrick's Day?" Sam shook his head. "It's crazy busy."

"What's your favorite Savannah story?" Carlita popped the last bite of crust in her mouth and reached for her glass of Coke.

"I have several favorites. The most popular ones with guests are the ghost stories. Since you're in the landlord business, I'll share the one about the Foley House."

"I heard about the Foley House, but not the history." Mercedes tore off a piece of her garlic knot. "I want to take the Foley House haunted tour one day."

"The Foley House is a great tour. I also recommend the haunted trolley tour that stops at the Parrot House Restaurant. It includes a behind-the-scenes tour of the underground passageways," Sam said.

"We already toured some of the tunnels," Carlita said. "In fact, we've got one under our pawnshop. It leads out to the river."

"Really?" Sam raised an eyebrow. "I would love to check it out someday."

Carlita and Mercedes exchanged a quick glance. "We sealed it off for safety reasons."

"I see." Sam didn't press the issue. "I best be getting to my storytelling, so I can earn my meal."

Sam's voice softened as he began to tell the tale of the Chippewa Square haunted house. According to Sam, the house was actually two joined structures. The eastern part was built in 1896 for Honoria Foley, the widow of a wealthy Irish immigrant.

"I've been by it many times," Carlita said. "It's a beautiful place."

"That it is," Sam agreed. "After The Great Fire of 1889 that decimated Savannah, Honoria decided to open her home as the first bed and breakfast in the area. Mrs. Foley saw great success with her inn and remained there until her passing."

"Where does the ghost story come in?" Mercedes asked.

"During renovations in 1987, workers tore down a wall and discovered a skeleton hidden inside. The remains have never been identified. Legend has it the poor guy had been murdered."

He went on to tell them that according to local lore, there were two versions of what happened to the unfortunate victim. The first was the man, a tenant, was enamored with Mrs. Foley, so enamored he snuck into her room one night. Startled, Honoria grabbed the nearest thing to her, a candleholder, and swung it with all of her might.

"That's terrible," Mercedes said. "Hopefully, the authorities realized it was an act of self-defense."

"Except the authorities never found out about it," Sam said. "The second version of the story is a boarder snuck into Mrs. Foley's room at night and tried to strangle her. In a panic to try to free herself, she grabbed a candlestick and bashed the man over the head, killing him instantly."

"She hid the body," Carlita guessed.

Sam nodded. "Most stories agree Mrs. Foley feared she would spend the rest of her days in prison, so she persuaded another tenant to help her hide the body. In return for his help and keeping quiet, he lived there rent-free. Supposedly, Mrs. Foley confessed to the misdeed on her deathbed, but never actually revealed where she hid the body."

"We know all about finding bodies in walls," Mercedes muttered.

Carlita nudged her daughter with her shoe and gave her a warning look. "The locals now believe the Foley House Inn is haunted?"

"And so do a lot of ghost seekers," Sam said. "The discovery and removal of the skeleton has triggered a haunting in Foley House. I've talked to several of the staff, who claim to have seen a male phantom in a top hat walking through the garden at night. There have been reports of strange noises and unexpected bursts of air that startle guests. Nicknamed 'Wally' by locals, the wraith shows no signs of checking out anytime soon."

"That's a good story," Mercedes said. "Now I really do want to check it out."

"Are there any more stories you'd like to share?" Carlita asked.

"I better save some in case you invite me over for dinner again." Sam grabbed his napkin and dabbed at the corners of his mouth. "The pizza was delicious and the company very much appreciated. I should head home. I've got some reservations to confirm and paperwork to take care of." He pushed his chair back and stood.

"Next time, I'll have you over for authentic Italian," Carlita promised. "Please take some of these leftovers with you. There's no way we can eat all of this pizza."

"Are you sure?"

Absolutely." Carlita hurried to the kitchen and grabbed a large Zip-lock bag. She stuck several pieces of pizza inside, along with a couple of leftover garlic knots and handed the bag to Sam.

"Thanks again, Mrs. Garlucci."

"Carlita."

"Carlita." Sam smiled warmly at Carlita, nodded at Mercedes and made his way out of the apartment.

After he left, Mercedes arranged the rest of the leftover pizza in one of the boxes and placed it inside the fridge. "I don't think he likes me."

"Whatever do you mean?" Carlita asked.

"He spent most of his time talking to you."

"Mercedes Garlucci." Carlita stuck her hand on her hip and studied her daughter. "That's crazy. He was talking to both of us. Besides, I thought you didn't like him."

"He's okay."

"He's very nice, not to mention handsome," Carlita said.

"If you like the tall, brooding hunky look."

"Ah...I get it." A slow smile spread across Carlita's face. "You *do* like him. That's the problem. You don't want to like him, but you do."

Mercedes face turned a tinge of pink. "That...that's crazy," she sputtered. "I do not think he's attractive or handsome. He's nice to you, but not to me."

Carlita threw her hands in the air. "I give up! First, he's rude and annoying and now he's indifferent. You definitely have the hots for our new tenant."

"I do not," Mercedes insisted. "That's absurd." She stomped out of the kitchen. Moments later, her bedroom door slammed.

"Oh, Mercedes." Carlita chuckled aloud. "It's starting to make perfect sense."

Chapter 19

Carlita studied the employment application and list of questions Pete had given her. The first applicant was scheduled to arrive any time and although she wasn't going to be actively participating in the interview, she planned to take a few notes to see if any of them might be a good fit for Ravello.

Pete had set up a small interview alcove in the main part of the pirate ship, what he explained would soon be transformed into the ship's snack bar and gift shop.

The ship would be advertised as a pirate ship adventure. Most of the action would take place on the open upper deck, where a band of merry pirates would engage in sword battle, shoot cannons and take prisoners, whose punishment was the threat of "walking the plank."

Gunner was also with them in the interview area, excited to be on board the ship. He walked back and forth along his perch, chatting with Carlita and Pete. "What a beautiful day to be walkin' the plank."

"Are you going to walk the plank, Gunner?" Carlita asked.

"Gunner is too handsome to walk the plank," he replied.

The first applicant arrived not long after Carlita. Pete's office assistant showed her in.

The nervous young woman perched on the edge of her seat, tightly clasping her hands in her lap.

Carlita was certain she was ready to bolt at any second and attempted to make her feel more comfortable. "What a beautiful day."

Gunner answered. "A beautiful day to walk the plank."

A small smile lifted the corner of the young woman's mouth when she noticed Gunner. "A talking parrot."

"Buenos días," he replied. "Gunner is handsome."

"Buenos días," the young girl replied.

"Usted entiende español," Pete said.

"Yes, I speak Spanish," the girl nodded.

A cold chill ran down Carlita's spine. She slowly turned to Pete, completely forgetting about the girl sitting in front of them. "You speak Spanish?"

"Aye. Tis always good for a pirate to speak a second language, especially when he's pilfering the islands, looking for booty."

"Looking for booty," Gunner mimicked.

Pete began going over the young woman's application, and Carlita attempted to keep up with the interview, but all she could hear were Kyle Flinch's words ringing in her head.

Her mouth went dry. Pete opening the pirate ship venture...Pete arguing with Lawson...Pete staying on the ship the night Lawson was attacked...Kyle overhearing Lawson and a stranger speaking Spanish.

She shot him a sideways glance. Had Pete attacked Lawson? Had he set fire to the Mystic Dream in an attempt to shut them down and eliminate the competition?

A sudden thought occurred to Carlita. What if Pete and Mark Fox were working together to oust Lawson? Neither man liked Lawson.

Pete turned to Carlita, a questioning look on his face and she knew he'd been talking to her.

"I'm sorry, Pete. I missed what you said."

"I asked if you have any specific questions for Sylvia."

"I do have one question."

Pete slid the application toward Carlita and she focused her attention on the paper. "I see you worked for Lawson Bates."

"Yes." Sylvia nodded. "I'm still employed, at least technically, although I have no idea what's going to happen now."

"I'm sorry to hear of Mr. Bates' injuries. How did you hear about us?"

"Luke Markham. He called a bunch of us to let us know you might be hiring," Sylvia said. "I was already looking for another job. I was making less than minimum wage and I could barely pay my bills. Mr. Bates kept bringing new people in for us to train. I was always one of the trainers because I speak Spanish."

Alarm bells went off in Carlita's head. "The new employees - they didn't speak English?"

"Not very many. One day we would have a new employee. The next it would be someone else. We were constantly training new people. We all complained to Lawson we didn't feel we

263

should have to train new employees all of the time. Nothing ever happened."

"I thought the employees were working on a petition to demand Lawson raise your wages or else," Carlita said.

Sylvia frowned. "No. A couple of us talked about it. As far as I know nothing was ever done."

"Do you know Kyle Flinch?" Carlita asked.

"Yeah. He didn't like Lawson either. He finally got fed up and quit."

Carlita scooched forward. "Kyle didn't bring a petition around for you to sign?"

"Nope."

"I think we've asked all of the questions we need to for now. Thank you for your time, Sylvia." Pete stood. "We'll get back with you in the next couple of days."

Pete led the woman from the office and returned with another potential employee.

The rest of the morning passed in a blur as several other applicants arrived. Most were either current or previous employees of Lawson Bates and almost all repeated the same story, that they were being paid less than minimum wage, a legal loophole since all of them worked in the restaurant industry and there was no regulated minimum wage.

They also complained of the high turnover of new employees who spoke no English. After the last applicant left, Pete settled in behind the desk. "What do you make of the interviews?"

"They all said pretty much the same thing. Subpar wages and high turnover rate of non-English speaking employees." Carlita drummed her fingers on the arm of her chair.

"Wait a minute!" She pulled her phone from her purse and scrolled through the pictures Autumn and Mercedes had taken while snooping around Lawson's office. "Autumn took a picture of the employee roster the other night." She looked up. "Do you have a copy?"

"Aye. I do. It's in my email." Pete turned his attention to his computer. He reached for his mouse and began clicking the button. "Here it 'tis."

Carlita slipped her reading glasses on and peered over Pete's shoulder. "I never paid much attention to this list. If you look at it, you'll notice something similar about each name on the list."

"They're all Spanish names. Look at the dates." Pete ran his finger along the screen. "Ten on this date. Then another eleven grouped together. Another ten after that. It's almost as if they're separated in segments."

"Meaning they didn't trickle in one at a time," Carlita murmured. A horrifying thought popped into Carlita's head. "What if Lawson Bates was involved in human trafficking?"

"The cousin of Savannah's mayor?" Pirate Pete frowned.

"He would be the perfect person to work the system. Think about it. He knows the ins and outs of the system. He could easily run up and down the coast, smuggling illegals in from Florida."

"Let me do a quick search." Pete grew silent as he tapped the keys. When he sucked in a sharp breath, Carlita knew they were onto something.

"You found something."

"Yes. There's a suspected human trafficking path. It leads from the Gulf and Caribbean, up through Florida. Savannah is the gateway north. It's called the Smuggling Straits."

Pete leaned in. "I found a story from late last year. It appears the Department of Homeland Security has been working hard to break up the trafficking ring and apprehend the major players. They've had some success in Florida."

"But not in Georgia," Carlita guessed.

"Not yet."

"Because Lawson Bates has connections."

"You're right. We may be onto something." Pete switched over to the list Autumn had photographed. "I'll have to see if I can track down a contact at the Department of Homeland Security."

"It's all falling into place," Carlita said. "The night the girls boarded the Mystic Dream, Mercedes could've sworn someone was on the riverboat with them. The cheap labor, the Spanish speaking employees and high turnover rate."

"Working short spurts of time and then disappearing," Pete said. "Could be one of the smuggled workers set fire and damaged the Mystic Dream."

"We've got to do something." Carlita popped out of the chair and began to pace. "We have to proceed with caution. Technically, we have nothing to go on - just our hunches."

"I agree," Pete said. "These are some very serious accusations."

"I'll do a little more digging around on my end." During the walk home, Carlita mulled over all of the clues. Mark Fox's trip to South America, how Glenda said Mark intended to confront Lawson and now Mark was walking with a visible limp. Was that the result of a confrontation with Lawson? Was Mark Fox involved in human trafficking?

She thought about Pirate Pete. Pete spoke Spanish, too. Pete had both motive and opportunity. He was guarding his pirate ship the same night Lawson was attacked. But why not confess to authorities if Lawson and he had become involved in a physical confrontation?

Could it be that Lawson threatened to make sure Pete or even Mark Fox never moved forward with their business ventures using his cousin, Mayor Puckett's, clout? Perhaps his real goal was to get them out of the way, fearing his human trafficking ring was in jeopardy.

She still hadn't been able to chat with Emmett Pridgen to get a feel for his involvement. The man was already a suspect in several suspicious business dealings in the Savannah area. What if he was involved in human trafficking?

Perhaps he was the one behind the scenes. From another previous investigation, she knew Pridgen was hot to get the gambling boat venture up and running.

What if Pridgen was determined to turn Pete and Lawson against one another in an attempt to get rid of the Mystic Dream riverboat *and* the new pirate ship venture?

Pridgen could succeed in eliminating the competition, clearing the way for the gambling boat!

She picked up the pace. There had to be a way to meet with Pridgen. Mercedes and she still hadn't heard back from the business development office on the bogus application for a graffiti art studio.

Mercedes was in her room when Carlita arrived home. She made a beeline for her daughter's bedroom and rapped lightly on the door.

The door flew open and Carlita stumbled back. "You got me again."

"Sorry, Ma. It's a bad habit." Mercedes leaned her hip against the doorframe. "How did it go with the interviews?"

"I think Pete and I figured out what's going on at Lawson's place. He's involved in human trafficking."

"What?" Mercedes' eyes widened. "Human trafficking?"

"Think about it...the low wages, the high turnover, and the unusual roster of names. Pete and I began to piece it all together. We think

Lawson has been smuggling people through what they call the Smuggling Straits. It's an undercover operation of smuggling illegals into the United States and using them for forced labor."

"Among other things," Mercedes said. "Remember how I said Autumn and I thought we heard someone on the Mystic Dream and then I thought I saw someone when I was getting off?"

"It could be illegals coming into the country," Carlita said. "Did you know Pete speaks fluent Spanish?"

"No and so does Mark Fox. Remember what Kyle said? He heard Lawson arguing with someone in Spanish."

"In his office," Carlita interrupted. "Where Autumn found the roster."

"And I heard noises and thought I saw someone." Mercedes pressed a hand to her throat. "We have to do something."

"I agree. Before we go to the authorities with nothing more than a hunch, I want to see if we can glean some clues from Emmett Pridgen. He could be part of this, too."

"The receptionist said we'd be contacted in forty-eight hours or less. I think we should call." Mercedes grabbed her cell phone off her desk and searched the internet until she found the telephone number for the business development office.

Using her best professional voice, she asked to speak with Emmett Pridgen about a business application. She paused as she listened to the woman on the other end. "I see. Okay. Thank you."

"Well?" Carlita asked.

"He's in the office and in a very important meeting."

"Crud."

"No, not crud." Mercedes squeezed past her mother and stepped into the hall. "We're going down to the business development office and plant ourselves in the waiting room until Pridgen gets out of his meeting."

Chapter 20

The same woman who was in the business development office the day Mercedes and her mother submitted the business application was there once again. She gave them a strange look when they walked in. "Can I help you?"

"Yes, we were in here the other day and filled out a business license application. You told us we would receive our answer within forty-eight hours or less, but we're kind of in a hurry."

"Our office has been very busy with applications this week," the woman apologized. "We're experiencing a slight backlog."

"I completely understand, but I have potential clients waiting to see samples of our graffiti products and I need an answer," Mercedes said. "If I recall correctly, you said the business development chairman, a Mr. Puckett..."

"Pridgen," the woman corrected. "Clarence Puckett is the mayor."

"Right. Mr. Pridgen would make the decision. I called a short time ago and you told me he was here, but in a meeting."

"That's correct." The woman nodded.

"Perfect. We'll wait over here until he's out of his meeting." Mercedes strode across the room to have a seat, positioning herself so that she was directly across from the reception desk.

Carlita settled into the seat next to her. "Hopefully, we won't have to wait too long." She reached for a copy of the *Savannah Today* magazine and began flipping through the pages while Mercedes turned her attention to her cell phone.

They sat for well over an hour before the receptionist made her way over. "You could be here for a long time."

"We're in no hurry," Mercedes said. "We have all of the time in the world."

"It's Saturday and we close at two o'clock."

Mercedes set her phone in her lap and gave the woman her full attention. "I intend to see Mr. Pridgen today if I have to stay past closing."

"Suit yourself." The woman marched back to her station, plunked down in her seat and frowned at Mercedes.

Mercedes returned the look.

"Whoever blinks first," Carlita muttered.

The sharp click of high heels drifted from the hall and two men, accompanied by a dark-haired woman, emerged.

Carlita immediately recognized one of the men as Pridgen, the same man she saw the night in the Black Stallion club during a recent stakeout.

The trio made their way to the door. Pridgen shook hands with both of them. "I'll be in touch early next week." He waited for them to exit the office before making his way to the reception desk.

"These ladies," the woman pointed to Mercedes and Carlita, "are waiting to have a word with you." The receptionist handed Pridgen a file folder. He flipped it open and then closed it before speaking to the woman in a low voice.

Pridgen tapped the tip of the file folder on the desk before slowly turning and making his way across the room.

"Mrs. Garlucci?"

"Yes." Carlita stood. "I'm Carlita Garlucci and this is my daughter, Mercedes."

"My receptionist, Debbie, told me you're anxious for an answer on your business application. We can go over it now. Follow me."

Pridgen didn't wait for a reply. He turned on his heel and began making his way down the hall. He stopped in front of an open door and motioned them inside. "Please have a seat."

"Thank you for taking the time to see us without an appointment." Carlita eased into the closest seat and Mercedes sat next to her.

"I see you're looking to open a..." Pridgen peered at the application. "Graffiti art studio." He flipped the application over. "You live in Walton Square?" He shifted his gaze, peering at Carlita over the top of the paper.

"Yes. We do," Mercedes said.

"And you already have several businesses...Savannah Swag Pawn Shop, you own several apartments, and you were just approved for a restaurant venture, Ravello, also located in Walton Square."

"That's correct," Carlita confirmed.

Pridgen dropped the sheet of paper and leaned back in his chair as he studied the women.

Carlita's first thought was that he was sizing her...sizing them up. "You bought the old Delmario place last year."

"Inherited," Carlita corrected.

"Inherited the Delmario property." Pridgen tapped the front of his chin with his middle finger. "I've heard your name before - Garlucci." The name rolled off Pridgen's tongue. "You moved here from New York."

"Queens to be exact. What does this have to do with our application?" Mercedes was beginning to lose her patience.

"Nothing really. Just curious. Rumor has it you're investing in Pete Taylor's pirate ship, which, by the way is currently on hold."

"I'm aware of that," Carlita said stiffly. "As my daughter pointed out, none of these things - my other businesses, my inherited property, our interest in opening a graphic art studio..."

"Graffiti," Mercedes interrupted. "Graffiti, not graphic."

"I find it intriguing a single woman would move to Savannah and start opening all sorts of different types of businesses, all within a relatively short period of time and all needing substantial amounts of capital."

"We're savvy businesswomen," Mercedes said. "Savvy enough not to put all of our eggs in one basket."

"Diversifying is always a smart business decision. I have a little friendly advice." Pridgen smiled, but the smile never reached his eyes. "Savannah is a small town with many area residents and business owners who have lived and worked here for generations. They take note of newcomers, especially ones who move down here from up north. Add to that the newcomers have wads of cash to invest. It piques the interest, if you know what I mean."

"It's no one's business where we get our money from," Mercedes snapped. "Those folks would be better off minding their own business."

Pridgen ignored Mercedes' rant. "As much as I would like to give you a definitive answer this afternoon, I'll need to gather some additional information, a better description of the business, along with projected income. Once I get the information, I'll present it to the business development's board of directors for final approval."

"Fine," Mercedes said. "We'll be happy to give you everything you need."

"I'll have Debbie at the front desk give you a second form you'll need to fill out." Pridgen stood - his signal the meeting was over.

Carlita began to panic. The meeting wasn't going as planned. She hoped to glean clues to figure out if Pridgen was involved in Lawson's attack.

Desperate to continue the conversation, she said the only thing she could think of to catch him off guard. "How is your casino boat project progressing?"

The question did the trick. Pridgen paused. "It's still in the planning stages. Are you asking because you're interested in partnering on that project, as well?"

"Maybe," Carlita fibbed.

"We have all the partners we need for the casino boat. If we decide to add more, we'll keep you in mind." Pridgen led them to the front desk. "Debbie, could you please give Mrs. Garlucci a copy of the business application *Form B*?"

"Of course."

Pridgen turned to Carlita and Mercedes. "I'll get back with you in the next week or so." He gave them a curt nod.

The receptionist handed Mercedes a sheet of paper and began explaining the form while Carlita watched Pridgen walk away.

Had Pridgen just threatened them that if they kept opening businesses in Savannah, certain area business owners and longtime residents would start snooping around in the Garlucci family past?

The thought made her dizzy. There were powerful people in Savannah...powerful people who might very well have connections to organized crime.

If the mafia up north caught wind of or even suspected Carlita had cash on hand, Castellini and maybe others would be on her doorstep demanding to have a look around, whether she wanted them to or not.

Carlita followed her daughter out of the office and they began making the trek home. "What do you make of Pridgen's comments?"

"I think he's a bully and he's trying to intimidate us," Mercedes said. "I ought to open up a graffiti art studio just to spite him."

"And graffiti what?" Carlita chuckled. "I know...you could start a business and call it Courtyard Art."

"The only problem is that I'm not artistically inclined."

"Practice makes perfect." Carlita linked arms with her daughter. "Maybe I'll join you. It could be very therapeutic."

"Have you decided what you're going to make for Cool Bones' courtyard get-together?"

"I was thinking of trying Tierney's marinara sauce recipe. Could you send me a copy?"

"You know what?' Mercedes abruptly stopped. "I don't think she's sent it to me yet. Let me check." She stepped off to the side and whipped out her cell phone. "Nope. The Ghost Roast is right around the corner."

"I'm running out of time. I would like to give it a kitchen test run first and tweak it to make it our own. Maybe we could swing by there to get a copy." The women turned left when they reached the corner.

The Ghost Roast was busy. Mercedes patted her stomach. "I'm kind of hungry. We should grab a bite to eat while we're here."

"Sounds good."

The hostess led them to a table near the front and handed each of them a menu.

Carlita perused the offerings. "I want to order Tierney's marinara sauce, so I can take it home to compare it with mine. Other than that, I think I'll go with the grilled fish after last night's pizza."

"Fried fish sounds good." Mercedes closed the menu and glanced around. "I see Tierney in the back. Here she comes."

The young restauranteur stopped by several tables before making her way to Mercedes and Carlita's table. "You again? Let me guess...you can't stay away from my secret marinara sauce." Tierney's eyes widened and she clamped a hand over her mouth. "I forgot, didn't I?"

"You did." Mercedes nodded. "It's okay."

"I had it ready to send and then forgot. I'll send you the recipe right now." She pulled her cell phone from her apron pocket and tapped the screen. "There. You should have it." She slipped the phone back into her pocket. "How is your investigation going?"

"It's not. We have too many suspects and not enough clues," Mercedes joked. "Even our friends are beginning to look suspicious."

"Kyle's information wasn't helpful?" Tierney asked.

"He gave us a big break when he told us about sneaking back on board the Mystic Dream and overhearing Lawson having a conversation with a man in Spanish. He said it sounded like a heated argument, but he didn't know what they were talking about."

"Because he couldn't hear what they were saying?"

"No." Mercedes shook her head. "Because he doesn't know Spanish."

Tierney snorted. "Kyle told you that? He speaks fluent Spanish. In fact, he lived in Mazatlán, Mexico for a couple of years before moving to Savannah."

Chapter 21

"Are...you sure?" Carlita asked.

"Of course. I'm positive." Tierney glanced across the restaurant and began motioning to someone. "There he is."

Kyle made his way over. "Hello, Mrs. Garlucci, Mercedes."

"Hello, Kyle." Carlita smiled back.

"We were discussing your conversation the other night. I hadn't heard the story about you sneaking back on board the Mystic Dream and overhearing Lawson speaking to someone in Spanish. Mercedes said you told them you couldn't understand what they were saying."

"No." Kyle shook his head. "I was on the other side of the door and they were speaking in low voices. I know they were speaking Spanish, though."

"But...but." Mercedes voice trailed off. Kyle *had* told them he couldn't understand what they were saying. In fact, he told them he heard two words and even looked one of them up...recoger.

Carlita tapped Mercedes under the table. "We must have misunderstood you, Kyle. It was such a long day and by the time we got here, I'm sure we were just confused."

"That's okay." Kyle swept his bangs off to the side. "How is your investigation going?"

"We have plenty of suspects, motives and opportunities, but haven't been able to figure out who attacked Lawson and damaged the Mystic Dream."

"Well, good luck." Kyle excused himself and made his way to the kitchen.

"I better get back to work, too," Tierney said. "The special today is the turkey club with chips for nine forty-nine."

"I think we're going to try the fish," Carlita said. "I also want an order of your marinara sauce to go."

"Good choice. The fish is delish. Sorry again about the recipe mix-up." She stepped over to another table and began talking to the diners.

"What do you think?" Carlita whispered.

"I think Kyle is lying." Mercedes covered her mouth. "We'll talk about it later."

The server made his way over to take their lunch order, which arrived hot and fast a short time later. While they ate, they discussed Emmett Pridgen.

"I think we should steer clear of him," Carlita said. "He could cause us some serious trouble."

"How? He doesn't know anything about us."

"But he has his suspicions," Carlita argued. "All it would take would be for a few nosy business owners to start snooping around. We don't need anyone from back home coming down here. We already have to deal with Vito."

"Vinnie sure dropped that bomb on our doorstep," Mercedes said.

"You know Pirate Pete speaks Spanish. Mark Fox speaks Spanish."

"Or maybe Kyle is lying and they weren't speaking Spanish. I'm beginning to suspect someone else is behind the attack," Mercedes said. "In fact, the more I think about it, the more I'm convinced the perpetrator is in plain sight."

"I hope we figure it out soon." Carlita polished off the last of her fish sandwich, left a small pile of fries behind and then slid her plate to the side. "Did you see John Alder put his place up for sale?"

"I did." Mercedes reached for a potato chip. "Have you heard why he's selling?"

"He's moving to California. He said he got a job offer he couldn't refuse." Carlita twisted her napkin around her finger. "I'll be sad to see him leave."

"I kinda thought in the beginning there was a spark between you two."

"Me, too, but we're just friends. I miss your father." Carlita swallowed hard. "He's been gone almost a year now."

"Yeah. I remember the day Pop died." Mercedes' lower lip started to tremble. "It was awful."

Carlita looked away as sudden tears burned the back of her eyes. There were moments it seemed like yesterday she made her vow to Vinnie on his deathbed to get their children out of the family.

Yet other times, it seemed so long ago...like a lifetime ago. Some days were easier than others. The hard ones brought her right back to the wrenching grief.

Her promise to Vinnie was one of the things that kept Carlita going, kept her pushing on. Admittedly, there were moments she wanted nothing more than to wallow in her own sorrow, but she made a promise and she intended to keep it...or die trying.

"You done good on keeping your promise to Pop."

"All except for Vinnie." Carlita dabbed at the corner of her eye. "I failed miserably."

"Did you, Ma?" Mercedes reached for her mother's hand. "You got a sweet new daughter-in-law and a new grandbaby on the way."

"Who also happens to be Vito Castellini's daughter."

"There's nothing we can do about Vinnie's new in-laws," Mercedes said. "Pop would be proud of you running your own businesses, making your own decisions."

"Learning how to drive his car?" Carlita smiled.

"He might have a thing or two to say about us not washing and waxing it every weekend," Mercedes joked.

"I'm sure he would."

"I'm no expert on love or romance," Mercedes said. "But I figure when your heart is ready to love someone again, you'll know it."

"You're right." Carlita reached for her purse. "We better get outta here. If not, we're gonna start bawlin' our eyes out. I'll go settle up at the cash register. On the way home, you can tell me who you think attacked Lawson Bates."

Mercedes waited outside while Carlita paid. "Can we make one more stop, Ma?"

"Sure. The exercise will do me good. I can burn off some of the food I ate."

The women changed direction and headed toward the river and the Mystic Dream, which was still moored in the same spot. Pete's pirate ship wasn't far away.

"I want to take a quick look at the Mystic Dream." Mercedes led the way, slowly walking along the sidewalk as she studied the riverboat.

"What are you looking for?" Carlita asked.

"Kyle Flinch mentioned that he snuck off the Mystic Dream by crawling through a broken galley window. I'm trying to figure out where it's at."

"There are some porthole windows near the front." Carlita pointed to the front of the riverboat.

"Those could be it," Mercedes said. "Kyle lied to us."

"I agree, but why?" Carlita paused in front of the wrought iron gate and stared at the Mystic Dream. "I just thought of something. When Pete and I were interviewing one of the Mystic Dream employees, she told us there was a high employee turnover and they were constantly training new employees and none of them spoke English."

"Which would fit in perfectly with the human trafficking angle," Mercedes said.

"But she said something else." Carlita shifted her feet. "Kyle mentioned he was working on a petition to demand better wages and he threatened Lawson with contacting the labor board. The employee we spoke with knew nothing about it."

"Maybe Lawson wasn't angry with Kyle because he complained about the wages," Mercedes theorized. "Maybe he was upset because Kyle found out about the trafficking ring."

"Because he overheard Lawson talking to a man in Spanish on board the boat," Carlita said.

"Motive and opportunity," Mercedes shoved her hands in her pockets. "Kyle was complaining about the wages. What if he became suspicious of the high turnover of Spanish speaking employees? He admitted he snuck back on the riverboat because he thought Lawson was up to something."

Carlita picked up. "He overheard Lawson working out another smuggling run to bring in more immigrants and then confronted Lawson. What if Kyle threatened to turn him in unless he started paying him hush money?"

"Kyle got ticked off, but with no way to prove Lawson was trafficking people up the coast, he was blowing hot air."

"He could've contacted the authorities to open an investigation," Carlita said. "Why wouldn't he do that?"

Mercedes rubbed her finger and thumb together. "Then he wouldn't make any more money."

"We could go back to *The Ghost Roast* and confront Kyle with our suspicions."

"And he would laugh right in our faces."
Mercedes tilted her head and gazed out at the
river. "I think I have an idea on how we can trick
Kyle into telling us whether he was involved in
Lawson's attack or the damage to the Mystic
Dream."

"What if it's not Kyle? What if it's Mark Fox or
Pirate Pete?" Carlita asked.

"That's a possibility," Mercedes said. "If so,
we're back to square one."

"I hope it's not Pete," Carlita muttered. "Not
only would I be a terrible judge of character, we
might be out twenty-five thousand dollars."

Chapter 22

"Before we do anything, we have to come up with an excuse to stop back by *The Ghost Roast*," Mercedes said.

"We got all the ingredients to make the marinara sauce. I say we whip up a batch, and then take it over to the restaurant for Tierney to sample our version."

"That's a great idea, Ma."

When they reached the apartment, they headed to the kitchen where mother and daughter whipped up a large batch of the marinara sauce in record time. Carlita made a few adjustments, tweaking the recipe so they weren't copying Tierney's exactly.

After several samples and taste tests, Mercedes proclaimed the sauce as tasty as Tierney's sauce.

Carlita placed a portion of the sauce in a small to-go container and then they headed back out. "Do you think we should stop by the police station first?"

"And tell them what? That we unlawfully boarded the Mystic Dream, broke into Lawson's office and found some paperwork we think points to his involvement in human trafficking?" Mercedes shook her head. "They'll laugh us right out of the building or arrest us."

"I suppose you're right. It doesn't help that Lawson is related to the mayor." Carlita picked up the pace to keep up with Mercedes' quick steps. "Do you think Tierney will be annoyed we keep dropping in?"

"She might. If you think about it, technically *Ravello* and *The Ghost Roast* will be competitors."

"I guess I wouldn't blame her," Carlita said. "I hope Kyle wasn't responsible for Lawson's attack."

"Me, too. Maybe it was Emmett Pridgen," Mercedes said. "He's a jerk."

"Better him than Mark Fox or Pirate Pete."

They reached the restaurant a short time later. It wasn't busy with the dinner crowd yet, and there were only a few patrons inside. Tierney was nowhere in sight, but Carlita caught a glimpse of Kyle in the back.

He gave a quick wave and then joined them near the front. "Tierney is off for a few hours. She won't be back until seven or so."

Mercedes held up the container of marinara sauce. "Ma and I made a batch of Tierney's marinara sauce, but with our own twist. We thought she might like to give it a taste."

"I'll leave it in the fridge for her." Kyle took the container.

"Thank you," Carlita said. "We were also going to give both of you some good news." She turned to Mercedes.

"Yes. We heard Lawson Bates is not only coming out of his coma, but he's also starting to remember what happened the other night and was able to give the authorities a vague description of his attacker."

The color drained from Kyle's face. "He did?" he squeaked.

"Yes. It's only a matter of time before the authorities find out who attacked him," Carlita said.

"And damaged the Mystic Dream."

Kyle's eyes grew wide and he took a step back. "That's...great news. I better get back to work." He lifted the container of sauce. "I'll be sure Tierney gets this." Without saying another word, Kyle darted to the back.

"Crud," Mercedes muttered. "I wanted to see the expression on his face when I described him as Lawson's attacker."

"Now what?"

"Maybe it's time to call Glenda and tell her the same story."

"I think we're chasing our tails," Carlita said. "Mark is as likely to confess as Kyle, if either of them is even guilty of attacking the man."

"Oh ye of little faith. We're just applying a little pressure to see if anyone cracks," Mercedes said. "Besides...nothing ventured, nothing gained."

"I suppose." Carlita stepped onto the sidewalk before dialing Glenda's number.

"Hello, Carlita. How are you?"

"I'm okay. I was talking to Mercedes. We heard Lawson has not only come out of his coma, but he's starting to remember details of his attack."

"Yes," Glenda said. "He is. Mark and I heard it's only a matter of time before Lawson is able to name his attacker. Mark's business partner visited Lawson a short time ago. He told us Lawson is very agitated, insisting the doctors release him from the hospital."

"I'm glad he's going to recover for everyone's sake and I'm sure the doctors are as anxious to have him leave as he is to go."

The women chatted for a few more moments before Glenda said she needed to take another call.

Mercedes watched her mother drop her phone into her purse. "What did she say?"

"I guess we weren't far off. Glenda actually heard Lawson is starting to recall details of his attack and is demanding he be released from the hospital."

"Perfect," Mercedes squealed. "Then this case will be solved soon and Pete can move forward with his pirate ship."

"Unless it's Pete," Carlita pointed out.

"Nah." Mercedes waved her hand. "It wasn't Pete. I'm still not convinced the person who damaged the Mystic Dream was the same person who attacked Lawson."

"I think it's the same person," Carlita said. "Who else could it be?"

"I keep thinking about the other night when Autumn and I snuck on board the Mystic Dream, how we were sure we heard something and then I was sure I saw someone on the top deck as we were getting off." Mercedes grabbed her mother's arm.

"Ma, what if those people, the trafficked people, are hiding out on the Mystic Dream? What if one of them accidentally set the fire?"

"Then we need to let the authorities know...in a roundabout way of course, without incriminating Autumn and you, that we suspect Lawson may be harboring/hiding illegals or individuals against their will on board the Mystic

Dream. A thorough search of the vessel while Lawson is still in the hospital would be necessary."

"If our suspicions are correct, he's probably desperate to get out of the hospital, before something else happens and his dirty little secret is uncovered," Mercedes said.

By the time they reached the police station, Carlita was out of breath and her calves were cramping in protest. Thankfully, there was a seating area. She eased onto the bench and began rubbing her legs.

Mercedes approached the station desk and briefly explained they needed to speak with someone who was investigating Lawson Bates' attack.

"I'll be back in a minute." The receptionist made her way out of the area and Mercedes began to pace.

Each second that passed was one second closer to Lawson getting out of the hospital and returning to the Mystic Dream.

Finally, an investigator who looked all too familiar emerged from the back and made his way over. "Mrs. Garlucci. I heard you and Mercedes were in the lobby and you wanted to discuss Lawson Bates' attack."

"Detective Polivich. Yes. We have what we believe may be some important information," Carlita said.

"Or at least we have some information about the investigation," Mercedes added.

"Mr. Bates is going to recover. In fact, he's raising a ruckus at the hospital, demanding he be released. I sent one of my guys over there to try to talk to him. I think he'll be able to name his attacker, if not today, then soon."

"He might not want to name his attacker," Mercedes said.

"Oh?" Detective Polivich raised an eyebrow. "Why?"

Instead of answering the detective's questions, Carlita asked one of her own. "Have you ever heard of the Smuggling Straits?"

"Of course. It's a smuggling operation that runs along the East Coast, north from Canada, all the way down to Florida and beyond. It's the nickname for the path the human traffickers use to transport people."

"We think Lawson Bates is involved in human trafficking." Mercedes quickly laid out their suspicions, starting with the damage to the Mystic Dream, the employee comments about the high turnover of riverboat employees who couldn't speak English, who were there one day and gone the next.

"That's all speculative," Polivich interrupted. "What proof do you have?"

Carlita and Mercedes exchanged a quick glance. "We were near the Mystic Dream the other night and thought we saw someone on board the ship, although it was shut down and all of the lights were off. And…there's something else."

Mercedes pulled her cell phone from her pocket, tapped the screen and then handed it to the detective. "I got this list from an anonymous source. It was in Lawson's office. Do you see anything unusual about the list?"

Polivich nodded grimly. "Yes. This looks similar to a list found during a recent human trafficking bust south of the Georgia border." He handed the phone back. "You're sure this was found in Lawson's office?"

"Yes. Positive."

"I don't know how my guys missed it," Polivich said. "I think it's time to get a search warrant for the Mystic Dream pronto."

*****

Mercedes pressed her hands to her cheeks as she watched Detective Polivich and several other investigators enter the Mystic Dream.

Carlita slipped in next to her daughter. "Do you think they'll find anyone?"

"Yes, I think so. If they don't, Polivich will never believe us again."

The women stood near the fence for what seemed like forever, but according to Carlita's watch, it was just over half an hour. "Maybe we should call the detective later instead of hanging around here. We could be waiting around all day."

"Not so fast. Check it out." Mercedes pointed to an ambulance entering the parking area. It drove past them and then parked in front of the Mystic Dream.

Two EMTs exited the vehicle. They removed a stretcher from the back and then followed an officer, who was guarding the entrance to the Mystic Dream, inside.

Moments later, a van arrived and pulled in next to the ambulance.

"Undercover police vehicle," Mercedes said.

"You think?"

"Yep. The license plates are government plates and I spotted a bubble in the dash."

"Ah. I didn't notice."

They waited a little longer and finally, several police officers emerged. They weren't alone.

Chapter 23

Along with the officers were half a dozen men and a woman. The woman and the men climbed into the van.

The EMTs emerged next, carrying a stretcher.

"I see someone on the stretcher," Carlita said.

One of the EMTs climbed in back with the person on the stretcher while the second one returned to the driver's side.

The ambulance pulled away and the van followed close behind.

Detective Polivich appeared and stood talking to the uniformed officer near the entrance.

"Let's go." Mercedes grabbed her mother's arm and hurried to the detective's side. "Well?"

"You were right. There were several immigrants hiding out in the engine room. It took some time, and the help of a translator, to coax them out. We promised we weren't going to place them under arrest."

"What about the ambulance?" Carlita asked.

"One of the men was badly burned. From what they told us, they accidentally set fire to the Mystic Dream and were too afraid to have the injured man go to the hospital for treatment," Polivich said.

"And Lawson didn't care enough about a human being to take him for treatment?" Carlita gasped. "What kind of person does that?"

"An evil one," Polivich said. "I'm on my way to confront Lawson now. He could still claim amnesia or that he has no idea what we're talking about."

"Do you think one of the men he was hiding attacked him?" Mercedes asked. "Not that I would blame them."

"They swear up and down they know nothing about Lawson's attack and appeared genuinely confused as to why Lawson hadn't returned. They were living in, to put it bluntly, squalid living conditions with limited food and bathroom facilities, not to mention sleeping quarters."

"There is one more person who might be able to shed a little light on Lawson's attack," Mercedes said.

"Who?"

"Kyle Flinch."

"We've already interviewed him. He was a former employee of Lawson's."

"I suspect Kyle may have known about the human trafficking and was taking hush money from Lawson to keep quiet," Mercedes said. "Our theory is they argued the other night and Kyle struck him."

She told the detective Kyle admitted to sneaking on board the ship and overhearing a conversation between Lawson and another man. "He claims they were speaking in Spanish and he didn't understand. We found out later Flinch speaks fluent Spanish."

Polivich jotted some notes in his notepad before flipping it shut and shoving it into his pocket. "If what you're saying is true, that he argued with Kyle over the human trafficking, Lawson is desperate to keep it quiet and won't name Kyle as his attacker."

"Which is what we told you before." Mercedes turned to her mother. "Now all we have to do is get the business development office to remove the hold on Pirate Pete's venture."

"I may be able to help," Detective Polivich said. "Let me make a couple of quick phone calls to see what I can do."

*****

The upbeat tempo of the jazz band drifted out of the courtyard and onto the sidewalk, where Carlita stood greeting guests. She recognized a few of the faces, but most of them, Cool Bones' friends, were people she'd never met before.

While she waited for more arrivals, she wandered over to admire the new sign Bob Lowman had hung above the door of her soon-to-be restaurant that morning. Carlita's chest swelled with pride.

"Tis a beautiful night," Pirate Pete's voice echoed in her ear.

Carlita was so absorbed in admiring her new sign; she hadn't heard Pirate Pete and Tori sneak up behind her. "It is," she beamed. "What do you think?"

"I think it's fabulous," Tori said. "I can't wait to enjoy some of your authentic Italian cuisine."

"This business is a dream come true." Carlita turned her attention to Pete. "Well? I heard the license went through and that Lawson is in jail awaiting a hearing for human trafficking. Perhaps you'll be in the market to buy a riverboat."

"I think not. I'm still trying to work out all of the kinks and get *The Flying Gunner* in open water."

"*The Flying Gunner*?" Carlita smiled. "Is that the name you picked for the ship?"

"Aye and Gunner is excited, squawking and carryin' on like he's something special," Pete said.

"Because Gunner is special. Now all you have to do is pick a name for your pirate show."

"Already got that figured out, too," Pete said. "It's going to be called *Pirates in Peril*. I've got a few of my workers already hired, thanks to a much-needed contribution by one of my favorite business partners."

"Hey," Tori tapped Pete's shoulder. "What am I?"

"My Queen Tori, of course," Pete winked at Tori. "With your generous contribution and a little number crunching, I'll have enough to get *The Flying Gunner* sailing the high seas in no time."

"It's a shame about Kyle Flinch," Carlita sobered. "And I feel terrible for his sister, Tierney."

"First, the authorities have to find him," Pete said. "Last I heard, they think he headed back to Mexico. I'm sure he's beginning to realize it wasn't worth taking money in exchange for compromising poor peoples' lives."

"Thanks to you and Mercedes, those people are free and maybe even more now that the authorities have tracked down some of Lawson's other connections," Tori said.

"I hope so. What a terrible situation."

The music grew louder and Mercedes flitted out of the courtyard. "There you are. Cool Bones is looking for you. He wants you to make a small speech."

"I hate public speaking," Carlita groaned.

"But you can mention Ravello," Mercedes argued.

"And the new pirate ship," Pete added.

"You guys are twisting my arm."

"In a good way," Mercedes said. "You got this, Ma. Remember, you're a savvy Savannah businesswoman."

Carlita chuckled. "You know what, Mercedes? I *am* a successful, savvy Savannah businesswoman." She clapped her hands. "Shall we go in and get this party started?"

Mercedes grinned. "Lead the way, Ma. Lead the way."

The end.

If you enjoyed reading "Pirates in Peril," please take a moment to leave a review. It would be greatly appreciated. Thank you.

Books in This Series

Made in Savannah Cozy Mystery Series

Key to Savannah: Book 1
Road to Savannah: Book 2
Justice in Savannah: Book 3
Swag in Savannah: Book 4
Trouble in Savannah: Book 5
Missing in Savannah: Book 6
Setup in Savannah: Book 7
Merry Masquerade: Book 8
The Family Affair: Book 9
Pirates in Peril: Book 10
Book 11: Coming Soon!
Made in Savannah Box Set I (Books 1-3)

Meet the Author

Hope loves to connect with her readers! Connect with her today!

Never miss another book deal! Text the word Books to 33222

Visit **hopecallaghan.com/newsletter** for special offers, free books, and soon-to-be-released books!

Pinterest:
https://www.pinterest.com/cozymysteriesauthor/

Facebook:
https://www.facebook.com/authorhopecallaghan

Hope Callaghan is an author who loves to write Christian books, especially Christian Mystery and Cozy Mystery books. She has written more than 50 mystery books (and counting) in five series.

In March 2017, Hope won a Mom's Choice Award for her book, "Key to Savannah," Book 1 in the Made in Savannah Cozy Mystery Series.

Born and raised in a small town in West Michigan, she now lives in Florida with her husband.

She is the proud mother of one daughter and a stepdaughter and stepson. When she's not doing the thing she loves best - writing books - she enjoys cooking, traveling and reading books.

Marinara Sauce Recipe

Ingredients:

2 (14.5 ounce) cans Italian stewed tomatoes

1 (6 ounce) can tomato paste

2 clove garlic, minced

1/8 cup green olives, minced

1 teaspoon dried oregano

1 teaspoon Italian seasoning

1 teaspoon brown sugar

1 teaspoon salt

1/4 teaspoon ground black pepper

3 tablespoons olive oil

1/3 cup finely diced onion

Directions:

In a food processor place Italian tomatoes, tomato paste, minced garlic, minced green olives, oregano, Italian seasoning, brown sugar, salt, and pepper. Blend until smooth.

In a large skillet over medium heat, sauté the finely chopped onion in olive oil for 2 minutes. Add the blended tomato sauce.

Simmer for 15 minutes, stirring occasionally.

Can be served as marinara sauce or as pasta sauce.

Made in the USA
Monee, IL
18 October 2021

80202782R10194